COVEN COVE

The House of the Rising Son

David Clark

1

"Just have a seat."

Several sets of hands ushered me inside to the closest chair. I fought each of them away. Despite the room spinning, I felt I was more than capable to find my way to the chair on my own. I was wrong, and would have completely landed on the floor if Jen hadn't caught me and moved me a few feet to the right to the chair that I never sat in as a child. It was one of those things that was nice to look at, but not something you sat on. A fact that made it a constant joke between my mother and father, but now I was sitting there, and the joke was on me. "How?"

The room was full of silent stares, but I felt a few struggling to withhold their sarcasm.

"If any one of you starts with the birds and the bees, I am throwing you in to the next state, and trust me I could do it." I held up a hand, showing one of my newest tricks. There wasn't just a glow. There were lines forming patterns and runes.

"I have heard of this before, and it is not that uncommon," said Theodora. She strutted across the room and sat on the loveseat that was next to the chair I sat on. She crossed her legs elegantly and leaned as close as she could to me. "The father is human, correct?"

I gave her a 'duh' look, and then I shot a warning at the rest of the room before anyone clarified he was human at the time. Nathan was no longer a member of the human species and was well on his way to becoming a vampire.

"That's a yes," assumed Theodora.

"I've heard about it too, but I've never seen it before," Marie said curiously. "It usually reversed, though. A human female carrying the child of a male vampire."

"That's true," agreed Theodora. She leaned back away from me and then looked at Marie Norton. The glance had a shared understanding between the two women. It reminded me of the days sitting in Mrs. Saxon's residence back in the coven, watching her and Jen or Mrs. Tenderschott carry on a conversation about me, but without me. Oh, to be back there. Those were simpler times.

"Everyone out," ordered Marie. "Everyone but Theodora, Jen, and Larissa. Everyone else get out now!" I had never seen or heard her this forceful before. She walked around and ushered a few stragglers out. Apryl tried to linger just outside the door, but Marie put a stop to that, and gave her a little shove from behind to move her down the hall.

"Larissa, I want you to relax."

That wasn't going to happen. I guess Theodora didn't know that I wasn't a relaxing type. Especially not with the world exploding around me, witches and vampires assembled outside, and the love of my life upstairs becoming a monster. Yep, there were plenty of reasons to relax.

"Can you feel it?" Marie asked.

Jen Bolden stepped into the center of the room and nodded.

Theodora nodded as well.

"What?" I screamed at them all.

Marie Norton walked over and kneeled in front of me. She laid her hands on my legs and looked up into my eyes the way she had for years. The look on my mother's face, or foster mother's face, was one of concern. Seeing it just added to my own. She then moved her hands up and over my stomach. I flinched backwards when she yanked her hands away from me and gasped. "It's there. I feel it. It has a pulse, but how?"

"Dhampir pregnancies have an accelerated gestation period. Some as short as a month," said Theodora. "But this is not one of those."

"Dhamp-what?" I asked. All I knew was that the word sounded both funny and terrifying at the same time.

Theodora leaned toward me again, and reached over with her long slender hands, taking mine in hers. "Forgive us Larissa. As strange as all this is for you to hear, it is also new to us. A Dhampir is what we call a child that comes from the union of a vampire and a human. No one knows why, at least not medically, but those pregnancies have a much shorter term. I have heard of ones as short as a month, and others a few months. I have never witnessed one personally, but..."

The three women exchanged looks again. I was beyond tired of this little unspoken language they had, and I leaned forward in my chair and allowed my head to drop into my hands. "But what?" I exclaimed. "Will someone tell me what is going on?"

"Larissa honey," started Marie Norton. "The problem is this is a little different. In those, the woman is human, not the other way around. That is a crucial difference. When we become vampires, our bodies stop changing. We stop aging. We stop growing. We stop everything. And... well, our bodies can't adapt to carry a child."

Maybe it was the stress of the situation, or the bizarre situation with everything else going on around us playing in my mind, but my first thought wasn't about what she had said and what it meant about my situation. My first thought was about the conversation I had had up on the rooftop one night, and I looked right at Jennifer Bolden and said, "Well, we have our answer." The last word passed my lips at the same time as the realization of what that answer meant entered my brain. The answer converted into a question. "Wait! If my body can't change. How can I give birth?"

"Yes," started Marie. "This leads to a ton of questions, and I don't have any answers," she finished, looking around at the others.

"I could try to ask around, but I'm not even sure who to start with," remarked Theodora. "It is possible this is a miracle of sorts."

Right then another wave hit me, and I leaped out of the chair and ran across the parlor and back out to the front porch, where again I heaved nothing more than a few strings of yellow foam.

"Dry heaves are the worst," Jen commented from behind me. I turned around and gave her the look from hell. She didn't know the half of it. I remembered dry heaves from when I was sick as a child once. The feeling of the gagging, and the constant rolling and squeezing of your stomach as it tries to empty whatever contents it had left. This was worse, way worse. The squeezing was there, with an enormous cramping that followed, almost paralyzing. Then came the heaving that felt like my stomach was being ripped from my insides.

"So, if everything happens faster, how long will this morning sickness last?" I asked, hoping to hear it would only be minutes, but then I heaved again in front of the large audience still gathered in front of the house.

Marie reached down and helped me gather myself, and then walked me back into the house with a supportive arm around my shoulders. We didn't stop at the parlor, and I let her guide me down the hallway to the kitchen where most of our new house guests were. A bit of dread set in. Was she wanting to make some grand announcement to everyone? I wasn't ready for this yet, not that most hadn't already heard Theodora's announcement on the porch earlier.

Amy pounced on me and grabbed me around my waist as soon as I entered the door. "Larissa, are you okay?" She squeezed me firmly, and I stroked her hair.

"I'm fine."

"You sure?" she asked, looking at me with her big blue eyes.

I nodded while I smiled and tried to be more convincing than I felt.

"I want to do a test," Marie said as she approached me with a glass of water in her hand. Apryl and Brad stared at the glass like the Wicked Witch of the West, fearful of melting. "Take a sip."

"What?" I asked in disbelief. "I've been dry heaving, and you want me to drink this?"

"Yes, I want to see something." She handed it to me.

"No thank you." I put the glass down on the table. "Are you trying to get me to vomit even more?"

"Larissa, trust me on this." Marie reached down and picked up the glass and gave me that look that only parents seem to have mastered. The type that told you they would not take no for an answer and would stand there until the end of time until you finally did what they wanted. For most, that wouldn't last more than a few minutes or maybe an hour at the most, if the parents were persistent. We were immortal, so that timeframe would be a little different.

I had done this a few times before. Some as an experiment when I was, I guess, what you would call–younger. Another when I made the mistake of swallowing after I brushed my teeth to freshen my breath. Just a few drops of water in my stomach caused a tossing and turning unlike anything I had ever felt, and then it rolled back up faster than the speed of sound, bringing up blood and anything else that might have been in there. I braced myself and took the glass, while looking at Marie for confirmation.

"Go on," she urged.

I tipped my head back, but stopped. My stomach was already turning. Either it was another dry heave coming or the anticipation of what was about to happen. To be on the safe side, I moved close to the backdoor. Pamela moved out of my way.

"What's going on?" asked Jack from the door.

"Larissa is about to spew," announced Apryl.

I didn't even bother with a dirty look or any comment. She was right. I was about to spew, but there had to be a point to this, or Marie wouldn't make such a request. I knew she wouldn't ask me anything that would be dangerous. She basically gave her own life to protect me. It was that trust that allowed me to raise the glass to my lips. It took a little more than that to tip it far enough for a few drops to pass over them.

Maybe it was curiosity. Maybe it was a lapse in judgment, but I did it. First a drop, then a second, and then what I guess most would consider a sip passed over my lips and into my mouth.

My lips clamped shut instinctively, and Pamela moved away even further from the back door.

"She's about blow!" Apryl warned, and everyone scattered.

It was cool and moist. A feeling of comfort flowed over and around my tongue on its way through my mouth, and a quenching of a thirst, that I didn't know I had, exploded when it hit my throat. That was it. After that, the feeling disappeared, and I braced myself for the rolling. My hands grabbed at my stomach, ready to hang on, but the loud gurgling I expected wasn't there. It was silent, really silent. It hadn't been that silent in almost a day. Then, amidst a room full of gasps and horrified looks, I took another sip, and after another uneventful reaction, I drank the entire glass, and then sat it down on the table.

2

After my little make-the-water-disappear-without-it coming-back-up trick, I left everyone down in the kitchen to examine the glass and prove to themselves it was just an ordinary glass. I wish it were as simple as a trick or magic, but I actually drank that water, and it tasted good. It was as simple as that. I wish what was upstairs was that simple as well, but it wasn't. Nathan wasn't just asleep, taking a nap, or playing some cruel joke on me. He was going through hell, no matter how peaceful he looked, laying there in my bed.

I went in and sat on one side of the bed. Jennifer Bolden sat on the other side. Her look answered the question I had. There had been no change, at least not outwardly. Changes were going on inside, and I felt it when I reached down and interlaced my fingers with his. He was cold, even to me. Gone was the warmth I so enjoyed feeling. Rough, almost paper-like, tissue had replaced the soft and supple feeling of his skin. This was temporary, but disturbing all the same. The light pulsation of fluid moving through his fingers was gone as well. They were now nothing but just gray fleshy protrusions off of his hand that laid limp between mine. I prayed to feel them move. Even a little flinch, or a stroke of one of his fingers against the side of mine like he did so often. It was a comforting sensation when he did it. Now, I wanted to be the one to give him the same comfort, so even though he felt lifeless, I kept on holding his hand with one hand while the other either stroked the back of the one I held, or I stroked his hair. I wanted him to know I was there. I needed him to know I was waiting for him when he finally wakes up.

All that comforted me was knowing at this moment he wasn't aware of what was going on. He already felt the worst of it, at least until he woke up. When it happens, you feel yourself die slowly, one part at a time. The pain of each adding on to the next, flooding your consciousness with nothing but an agony that pushes out any chance of seeing your life flash before your eyes. There is no room for thoughts of loved ones that may miss you, or ones you know you will miss. There is no time for thoughts of regret. The only flash you see is when the light disappeared and the blackness takes hold, and then it's all gone.

I don't really remember anything of when I was out. If it felt like I was sleeping, I don't know. I just wasn't there, and then I woke up with no sense of how much time had passed. Had it been minutes, hours, or days? I didn't know. I didn't care.

What I felt was a was an insatiable burning deep inside and Marie ran me out the backdoor to the woods behind our house to help me take care of it.

"You know, Gwen would just die if she knew you were pregnant with his child," remarked Jen.

I looked up in shock and quickly held a finger over my lips, urging her to keep it quiet.

She looked back at Nathan. "He can't hear us."

She was right, and I knew it, but that didn't make talking about him or things like that in front of him any less weirder. My mind told me he was still there, and I rubbed his hand as an apology for being so callous. Then I smirked.

"You know I'm right."

"Yes, you are," I admitted, not taking my eyes off of Nathan this time. "I didn't think you thought about things like that. Apryl? Yes. You? No."

"I would be lying if I didn't say that prima donna witch didn't get on my nerves more than a few times. I am sure she is sitting up in the coven enjoying the fact that everyone but the witches were exiled."

"Probably buddy-ing up to Mrs. Saxon..." then a question hit me, and I turned to look right at Jen. "Jen, she is still in charge of the coven, right? Please tell me she is."

"Yes, why do you ask?"

My shoulders slouched. "They threatened to take it from her before because of me, and now all this. It kind of proved all the points Mrs. Wintercrest tried to make back in those trials." My voice trailed off as I imagined them removing her.

"Stop!" ordered Jen. "None of this is your fault. Not a single thing... and, if you really think about it, Rebecca kicking all of us out probably helped her standing with the council. That Mrs. Wintercrest was there with a few others just before Rebecca told us to leave."

"Maybe," I said, unsure if I really believed her or not.

"Demius and Mrs. Tenderschott tried to talk her out of it, but she refused to even listen to them. The council members that were there agreed with her actions. I wouldn't be too worried."

"Okay," I said, but I still wasn't sure. I could see Mrs. Saxon being so upset over Nathan that she threw everyone out, but I could also see her being forced to by the council. Either was plausible. Which was the truth? Only Mrs. Saxon would know. I knew her well enough to know she would put up a strong showing either way. If it was all her, I couldn't blame her. A shudder went through my body when I thought of what I had cost her, and it had nothing to do about my suspicions about the coven. Nathan was her everything, thus the unwritten rules, which I had broken every single one I knew about, and probably several I hadn't heard of yet. There was something extra vile about that thought. Could it be? I had only found out I was pregnant a few hours ago. Was I already seeing things differently?

"Don't do that to yourself."

"I'm fine."

"No, you're not. I see that look on your face, and I know what's running through your head. Now stop it." She leaned across the bed and placed a hand on my shoulder. "Focus on what is in front of you right now. Don't worry about the past. Nathan will need you, and well… you need to stay calm for your little one."

My free hand reached up and instinctively rubbed my stomach. I could have sworn it felt different. A little bigger. Was it even possible? In just a few hours?

"You know, I've been giving your situation a little thought. I think it's his fault." She nodded her head in Nathan's direction.

There was no way she was that naïve. She was older than me, at least physically, and she was married. She was the one that offered to have the conversation about the birds and the bees with me. I gave her my best 'duh' look back.

"No, I mean about how it happened."

Again, I gave the same reaction. There was no other suitable response.

"Not like that," she corrected. "Everything they were talking about downstairs involved a human female, which makes sense. Her body can make the adjustments to carry a child to term, and ours can't, but we are missing one factor about you and Nathan. You're a witch and his mother is one too. Who's to say Nathan doesn't have a little in him that manifested this way? It's a big unknown in the equation we can't ignore."

"Can it do that?" I asked, and then spouted out another question. "Oh, you don't think…"

"What? I don't think maybe Rebecca lied to everyone, including Nathan, to protect him?" Jen shrugged her shoulders and scrunched her face up. "Anything's possible. She is a very private woman when it comes to her husband, and as you know better than ever, very protective of her son."

Looking back at things, she was right to be protective, and the idea Jen had just floated was possible, but not all that probable. Magic had a way of making itself known. If Nathan had anything in him, it would have, should have, come out by now, even accidentally. A random thought that triggered something to happen–like throwing an annoying classmate in the pool. An event that still brought a smirk to my face. Even something simple, like something magically materialized out of thin air. Anything at all. Maybe it had. I had only known Nathan for a relatively short time. Even by human standards, it had only been just a few months.

I looked back at his blank face, and wondered, could he be hiding something from me? The thought prompted a quick headshake. We didn't have secrets. Well, I didn't have any secrets I kept from him. That was a promise I made to him after I snuck out looking for Marie, and I kept it. Then the list of situations that had I kept from Nathan played in my mind, prompting a feeling of guilt. I didn't really like it. I had a reason for not telling him each and every time. They weren't exactly secrets. I was just delaying when I told him. That attempt at rationalization did nothing to squash my guilty feeling. The situation with Clay wasn't really something I was delaying when I told Nathan. I didn't know how to tell him, and really just hoped it went away on its own. It didn't, and then it blew up right in my face. Whether I would have ever told Nathan, I wasn't sure. It was another hit to the fabric of who I thought I was. I thought I was an honest and open person with the man I loved, but in reality, I wasn't. I was a briar patch of rationalization and selective openness. They say strong relationships are built on a foundation of truth, and I hadn't really held up my end of things. Was it possible he wasn't either?

"What secrets are you hiding?" I whispered, and then reached up with my free hand to caress his cheek.

"Don't do that to yourself, Larissa. I see those wheels turning."

"It was just a question."

"No, it wasn't," remarked Jen. "I know you. You have probably already analyzed every moment you and Nathan spent together for any signs that you might have missed and any times you think he may have tried to mislead you, and wait..." she held up a finger as soon as I opened my mouth. "You also went through every time you haven't been completely truthful with him. Just stop and wait for him to wake up. Then, when the time is right, ask him. Considering the situation," she glanced down at my lap. "I am sure he will understand and will answer honestly, if he knows."

"Too bad we don't have those stones Mrs. Tenderschott has. I could put one in his hand right now."

"You could. You could walk out to any of those witches that are camped outside and ask them if they have something like that. Your Master Thomas probably could find something like that if you asked, or you could show Nathan some trust, and just wait. Which is what I would do, if you want this old woman's opinion."

"I'm older," I snipped back

"You know what I mean."

"Yep," I agreed. She was giving me relationship advice, and she was absolutely more experienced there than I was. "Oh, guess what happened downstairs after you came up? You'll love this. Marie had me drink a glass of water, and I didn't vomit."

"A whole glass. Not just a sip?"

"A whole glass, and it tasted good."

Jen regarded me with a curious and concerned look. Without warning, she reached across the bed and yanked my hand away from Nathan's and held it in her own palm up. Her thumb pressed hard into my wrist and then she waited.

"Jen, what are you…"

"Quiet," she snapped. Her thumb searched, and then she released me. "No pulse. You're still one of us."

"I could have told you that," I said and yanked my hand back.

"Your child is all human, though. It has a strong rhythm."

"Why can't I feel that like everyone else?"

"Remember when you first arrived at the coven? You were a girl of mystery. You still are."

If there was anything within an arm's reach, I would have thrown it at her, and conjuring something took too much energy at the moment. I didn't want to be that girl anymore. All that mystery was tiring and stressful. Oh, how much I desired to just be normal.

"How is he?" asked Lisa from the doorway. She was bracing herself with one hand, the other arm wrapped around her ribs.

"Lisa, you need to go get some rest."

Lisa didn't follow my orders and stumbled into the room and over to the side of the bed, where she gingerly sat down next to Jen.

"He is fine, and you need to get back to bed and rest. Kevin believes at least one of your ribs is broken."

"I don't doubt that." She groaned as she shifted around on the bed to get comfortable.

She looked at Nathan the same way everyone did when they saw him lying there; like they were looking at a dead body. If I hated people looking at me with pity, I morally despised anyone looking at Nathan that way, and I had to remind anyone who wasn't a vampire that he wasn't dead. That didn't stop the looks. Neither did my attempt to banish everyone. Everyone continued to stop by to check on him.

"So how much longer will he be like that?"

"Hard to say. It's different for everyone," explained Jennifer. "The biggest change is done. Now his body is preparing for its new state."

"Larissa," Jack called from the door. I was about to spin around and tell him no more visitors. I wanted Nathan to be left alone. "Master Thomas needs to talk to you downstairs for a minute."

With no hesitation, I declined. "I will be down there once Nathan is awake."

Jack took a step back from the door, but then stepped back to the door and added, "He was rather insistent."

I was about to become rather insistent myself when Jen looked over and said, "Go on. Lisa and I can watch over Nathan."

"All right, but come get me if anything happens." I stood up but waited for a response before I moved.

"Absolutely."

I took one more look at Nathan before I slowly walked to the door.

"Hey Larissa, is it true?" asked Lisa. She rubbed her stomach with one hand. I nodded, and Lisa smiled. "I'm glad. Gwen would have a cow if she knew."

"Why does everyone keep saying that?" I asked rhetorically.

"She'd have a whole dairy farm," remarked Jack as I passed him going out the door and down the stairs. Now that got a smile from me.

3

"Master Thomas," I called from halfway down the stairs.

"How is young Nathan?" he asked from where he stood down in the foyer.

"No change," I said.

"How are you feeling?" he asked, brushing right past my response about Nathan as if he didn't really care and was only asking to be polite.

It irked me a little and caused my answer to be abrupt. "Fine."

"Good, I have someone you need to meet." Master Thomas turned and walked out the front door without another word. Leaving to assume I was to follow him.

We walked out the door, and off the porch across my battle scarred yard. The yellow line of runes I had put there yesterday was still present. The bright intensity of the line prompted a small smile as we crossed it.

Just beyond it were two camps. Opposing armies, it appeared. These weren't the Union and the Confederate armies camped before a great battle. Though one occurred here on this very property many years before I was born, or so my grandfather told me. On one side, there was a camp of vampires that hung back close to the trees. They lurked in the shadows, which completed the image that most of the world had of us. We weren't heading in their direction. We were going to the other side, but that didn't mean the vampires weren't taking notice of our presence.

Where we were heading resembled something of a circus or a fair. Some had put up tents, but everywhere you looked small campfires burned, with several people gathered around them for warmth. Some played instruments like guitars or flutes, while others sang and danced. They all looked in our direction as we passed. Most gave a respectful nod to Master Thomas. It was an understandable acknowledgement of respect considering who he was. I, on the other hand, received looks of indifference from those that ventured close enough to look me in the eye. Many seemed leery of me and only looked in my general direction.

Master Thomas stopped at one tent, and I stayed a few steps behind him. "Is he in?" he asked.

"Yes, but not for you," answered the man, who was slightly taller than Master Thomas, and also a lot thinner. He looked like a human skeleton with a black robe draped over it. Only his face with pronounced cheekbones and a scruffy beard were visible beneath its hood.. He stepped to the right, moving his thin frame in between Master Thomas and the tent. The two men were inches from each other, and the aggressive stranger's jaw twitched. Master Thomas was his usual statue of stoic calm.

"Let him in," called a voice from inside the tent.

"Maybe next time," grumbled the thin man, and he stepped aside, letting Master Thomas pass by. When I stepped forward, he took an aggressive step toward me. I grinned, showing the points of my fangs. Not that my black eyes weren't a dead giveaway. He returned a similar grin, and I searched his eyes for the familiar emptiness, but what I found were bright brown eyes with flecks of gold glittering in them. I had seen that only three times before. The first was when Mr. Markinson knocked me unconscious outside the coven.

"Larissa, come on," Master Thomas called, holding open the tent's cloth door. I stepped through and expected to see the inside of a small tent, but this was not like any tent I had ever seen before. It was rather spacious. I needed to learn to drop any expectations of the world and just go with the flow. Stepping in through those dilapidated doors and into the coven should have taught me that. At the other end of this room, across the white oak hardwood floors, and behind the burgundy sofa stood a rather regal looking man, or so he seemed from behind. He wore some type of black cap with locks of black curly hair protruding out from under it.

"Guard dogs?" asked Master Thomas.

"One can never be too careful, Ben." He turned around holding a coffee cup, and my mouth dropped open. The man was gorgeous. I mean Greek god gorgeous with striking facial features chiseled from stone. His striking blue eyes were an exotic contrast to his dark complexion and jet-black beard and hair.

"You," he said, regarding me. "I must commend you. You are either somebody, or just somebody with a death wish with how you went after Madame Wintercrest. I applaud your audacity, and your stupidity." He held up his coffee cup as a toast. "Would you like some coffee? I grow my own beans." He motioned to the windows behind him, where a field of coffee plants stretched as far as the eye could see up and over a distant hill.

"Oh, she's somebody," remarked Master Thomas.

Our host put his cup down on a table and walked around the red couch, and approached me, taking a better look. I felt like a bug under a microscope. "I see," he said curiously, and then pointed right at me and asked Master Thomas, "Is this her?"

"It is. Marcus Meridian meet Larissa Dubois." Master Thomas handled the introductions.

"So, you're the one that this old folk keeps babbling about. The one that can help restore the natural order of things." He reached out and offered his hand.

My hand trembled all the way to meet his. I was more than a little star struck. That name was one that any witch would, or should, recognize. I did as soon as

Master Thomas said it. "You're a M-M-Meridian," I stuttered, and was too shocked to even care.

"The last time I checked my driver's license, I was." He let go of my hand, but mine hung there in the air.

"I don't understand," I said, and tried to pull myself together. The tremble was gone, but the realization I was standing here in front of a Meridian still had me out of sorts. I wasn't sure if I should bow or something.

"What's not to understand? This is my castle."

Master Thomas chuckled. "No, she means why you are here, among the rogue elements?"

Marcus smiled, and I felt the world light up around me. "That's both a funny story and one that is not that interesting." He walked back to the table he placed his coffee cup on and picked it up, taking a sip. "You aren't the only one who isn't on the best of terms with Wintercrest, or the rest of the council. Let's just say several generations back, my family had a difference of opinions with most, if not all, of the council, and we now find ourselves on different sides."

"That is putting it mildly," said Master Thomas. He moved forward and took a seat on the couch, and did so without an invitation. I found that odd considering we were guests, and who our host was. It was almost like he was comfortable. "Your great grandfather was called a heretic. Do I have the term right?"

"You do," agreed Marcus Meridian. He sat on the other end of the couch and sipped at his coffee. He crossed his legs and sat back casually.

"They even wanted to do that ceremony to strip your family of any magic. Do I have that right?"

"Yes, I guess." Marcius Meridian dismissed the question flippantly with a hand. We were talking about a stain on his family's history. An event that forced a great family, make that one of the greatest families in our world, into a disgraceful hiding. I knew the name. We all talked about it with the reverence of a royal family, and, in every sense of the word, they were royalty. There weren't any true kings or queens of the witches, but there were those dynasties that sat atop the council for generations. Those families whose names became synonymous with greatness; the target for what everyone should strive to be. This should be akin to sacrilege, like criticizing the Pope, but yet I was here watching Master Thomas do it with no hesitation. "To be true, I doubt that ceremony works, anyway. I believe it is more of a pomp and circumstance thing."

"Probably so," responded Master Thomas. "And help me remember, there was a single family that stepped up to stop it."

Marcus nodded.

"What was their name? Do you remember?" prompted Master Thomas. He was egging him on. I could tell by the way he looked at him, but I didn't understand why.

"Larissa, why don't you take a seat in that chair behind you? I have a feeling we are going to be here for a while."

I was about to point out there was no chair, but when I turned out of the way so Marcus could see, there it was, just a few feet behind me, a red velvet chair. It wasn't there when we first came in. I knew that was a fact. I would have stumbled over it if it had been. I sat down as nonchalantly as possible.

"So, Marcus, do you remember the name of the family that helped you? The family one might say you owe a little debt to."

Marcus Meridian looked away from Master Thomas and exhaled. "Are we really doing this?" His head jerked back toward Master Thomas, and he looked at him sternly, almost like a warning.

"We are."

"Fine. Fine." He resigned himself and stood up and walked around the couch back to the table he was standing at when I and Master Thomas first entered. He picked up a square bottle of brown liquid and popped off the top before pouring a liberal amount of the libation into his coffee. "If you are going to ask me to go through all the sordid details of my family, then I am going to need something stronger than this coffee." He gave his coffee a little stir with a finger and then leaned back against the table, facing us.

"Where to start? Where to start? My family disagreed with the direction the council was taking. Their purpose was changing pretty drastically. One might say it was a one-hundred-and-eighty switch. They were no longer a group focused on protecting and teaching our kind. They wanted to govern and control. Something they were never meant to do. The council's single purpose back then was helping and assisting. It was to bring our community closer together. I will tell you what I heard my grandfather say once." Marcus stopped and took another healthy swig of his drink.

"The world was expanding. The new world was growing in size every day, and life was changing in so many ways. Things such as religion and beliefs were taking a back seat to prosperity and drive. Where your life *was* focused on community and helping others, now it became all about the person. We, as a people, and I mean the larger group of humanity, were losing everything that made us great, everything that made us strong. Our community of witches wasn't immune to this, and it was more important than ever to focus on our people. To continue to help one another. To continue to teach and pass down our identity, but the modern plague took hold, and many of our people saw their position on the council not as a responsibility to help, but as an opportunity to rise up and place themselves above all others, and then just to be safe, they set rules in place to make sure they stayed there for generations. Before, they granted your seat on the council based on the works you performed, not what you could do. Then the whole thing shifted to protecting your seat, which meant corruption, and..." Marcus exploded forward, and leaned against the back of the couch. "Larissa, have you ever read Plato's Republic? It really is a wonderful book about the search for the truth. Have you read it?"

I had more than read it. My father assigned it to me one winter to read. It was more than a suggestion. Every night we talked about what I had read, and what I felt it meant, and what it meant about life. At no other time had my father ever assigned me anything like that before, or taken such an interest. That included magic. My mother did most of the drilling where that came, but to my father, this seemed important and now the pieces of the puzzle of why fell into place. "Yes, my father had me read it."

"And what did you take away from it?"

This was a simple question. There are four points I remembered more than any other my father and I discussed. We discussed these four over and over again and even continued to do so long after I finished reading the book. "The importance of being just and true."

"Yes, but what does it say about leaders? He has some very specific tenets. Do you remember them?"

Did I remember them? I had them drilled into me. There was no doubt about that. "A true leader should always keep an eye on tomorrow, share it, and drive toward it. That vision should be realistic and achievable. This was what my father called avoiding setting yourself up to fail. Another point he often reminded me from the text was a leader should always think of themselves as a teacher and a learner. That a person with knowledge to pass on who does, or believes there is nothing left to learn, is a fool. And to be wary of the leader that wants to be a leader. A leader should be truly altruistic. We should question anyone who is driven to seek power."

Master Thomas gave a polite and quiet clap.

"Very good. Your father taught you well," said Marcus Meridian. He let go of the couch and walked around it, retaking his seat. "Would it surprise either of you to know the council was failing on all of those points?"

That answer for me would be an emphatic no. After my recent involvement with the council, it wouldn't surprise me in the least.

"That is what my great grandfather saw, and he pushed back harshly. He challenged them. He challenged every one of them," Marcus said forcefully. He appeared agitated and had ignored his coffee and its additive. Perhaps he needed a little shot of it to calm down. He was making me uncomfortable, but Master Thomas appeared to be as cool as a cucumber, sitting there listening. I knew him. He had an end in mind, and this was all part of the path. That was how he worked. What the end was here, I didn't know yet. "What did they do? How did they react? They accused him of creating a schism and took him into custody and threatened to strip him of all of his magic, sending shockwaves through the others that felt the same way forcing them into silence."

"Can they do that?" I blurted.

"Do what?" asked Marcus.

"Take away someone's magic."

Master Thomas leaned forward and held up a hand toward Marcus, cutting off his attempt to answer. "I'm not sure. They say there is a spell that can strip it away, but I have never seen it and it has never been used, to my knowledge. Not that the threat isn't, or its possible existence isn't, an effective deterrence to keep people in line. Luckily for Marcus's family there, someone stepped in to help. Didn't they?"

Marcus groaned and looked away.

"What was their name?" Master Thomas asked again. He leaned toward Marcus Meridian to urge his answer to emerge. I wondered what was so important about the name. There was one option, though my mind had already considered, and the more I thought about it, the more it made sense. The family name had to be Wintercrest. They spared his family in a show of mercy, and instead, just exiled him. I was sure that would earn them a substantial amount of respect, and probably helped her family rise to the position they had.

"Dubois," muttered Marcus.

I was still working over the thought that it was Wintercrest when I heard my own. My body jerked up straighter than I normally sat, and my head cocked to one side as I stared right at Marcus with my black eyes.

"Yes Larissa, it was your grandparents that saved the great and powerful Meridians. You have never heard that story, have you?"

I shook my head, still too shocked to talk. The Meridians were legends in our world. They were the Supremes of the Supremes, but never held the role by their own choice, which made them even that much more legendary. My family knew them. They not only knew them, but they also helped them.

"Well, they did, and the way I see it, he owes you a debt of gratitude."

"Next time you see your grandparents, tell them thank you." Then it was his turn to stop and look surprised. "Wait, the math doesn't work." He held out his hand and a bright light with blue sparks hit me, causing my skin to tingle. He watched intently as it moved up and down me, then he got up and walked closer, trying again. It didn't hurt. It wasn't even annoying, but I still didn't like it and was ready to get up and do something above it, Meridian or not, but he stopped before he pushed me over the edge. "This isn't a trick?" he asked, now looking at Master Thomas.

"No trick.

"The math still doesn't work," he proclaimed.

"Oh, it works. You should know your history, and should be more observant. Look closer," urged Master Thomas, and Marcus Meridian did just that. He looked closely, and again I was not a fan, and grew more uncomfortable by the second, but again he stopped just in time. This time he jumped backward, and I saw a glow start in his hands.

"Don't try it," I stood up in a blink, and warned. "I will have you against the wall before you can raise your hands."

"Knock it off, both of you," Master Thomas bellowed. "Marcus, yes, she is a vampire, but not what you are thinking. She is also a witch. And she is the answer to all of this."

"The answer?" asked Marcus Meridian. He stood poised to attack me, but hadn't. I wasn't sure if it was my warning or Master Thomas's request, but I hadn't dropped my guard yet. He would have to make the first move either way. "What the hell is the damn question?"

"Is she the same girl in that picture of your grandfather back there on the table? She is." Master Thomas sat calmly, almost smugly, while Marcus jumped over the back of his couch and retrieved a large golden picture frame. I couldn't see the picture in the frame, just the back side of it, but I had a clear view of how intensely his eyes studied the picture, and then studied me.

"This... is you?" He turned it around so I could finally see it. Even from where I sat, I could see it clearly and recognized the grainy black-and-white photo of my family and the Meridians standing outside our house. I think I was eight there. This was one moment my mother didn't hesitate to remind Mrs. Landry of often.

"It is. I was eight."

"Impossible!" Marcus took another look at the picture, and then a look at me.

"Jean and his followers turned her eight years after that picture was taken. So, she is now a vampire, who retained her abilities as a witch." Master Thomas reached over the back of the couch and took the photo from the slack jawed Marcus Meridian. He put it back in its original place. "Which means she is also the answer to the question your grandfather was trying to answer."

Marcus attempted to say something once or twice, but no sound came out. His eyes took a few side glances at me, and then down at the picture. There was comfort in seeing that. It meant I wasn't the only one confused as hell by what was going on.

"That is where your debt comes in." Master Thomas got up off the couch and walked around to the table where the coffee was. "I think I will have some. Would either of you care for some? Marcus, can I freshen your cup?" he rattled the bottle that Marcus poured into his coffee.

"My debt? I think I get it." He looked right at me as compassionately as anyone had looked at me in a long time. Maybe since Mrs. Saxon did that first night in the coven. "I heard what happened to your betrothed, and I am sorry to tell you, I can't help you. Only one substance can reverse vampire venom, and I'm afraid yours is still red." He pointed at the blood charm dangling from my neck.

"She knows that, and if there was a spell or a potion to reverse it, trust me, she would have already done just that. In many ways, she is far more powerful than you. Just a little unrefined, but we have been working on it." The spoon Master Thomas stirred his coffee with rattled against the cup as he stirred, and his last comment stirred me. I was unrefined?

"Then," Marcus threw his arms up and bobbled his head. "What is it Ben? What do you need from me?"

"I want you to help me train her. Help me refine her."

"Why?"

"Because she can fix it all."

4

Marcus Meridian and Master Thomas talked about what *ALL* meant for the rest of the morning. I just listened as neither really asked me to contribute. I was the thing in the room that they talked about and pointed to as a piece of evidence in some presentation before a court. At times it appeared the court accepted the argument and at other times there were objections. Those objections created other conversations. When logic appeared to fail to sway Marcus, Master Thomas threw on the weight of his family debt to my family, tipping the scale back in his direction.

"I thought you were my teacher," I said on the way back up to my house.

"I am, but I will need help, and his involvement will go a long way toward your acceptance," replied Master Thomas.

"My acceptance?"

"Larissa, this goes far beyond magic." The porch floorboards creaked as we both stepped up on them, and that sound brought a thundering herd through the door to meet us.

Mike and Apryl both tried to fit through the door at the same time, bumping and jostling each other. Apryl eventually won and knocked Mike out of the way and grabbed my hand.

"Come. Hurry. It's happening," Apryl blurted. She grabbed my hand and yanked me hard through the doors and up the stairs.

Rob and his brothers stood at the bottom of the stairs and appeared to be on edge. Laura held Amy. Both had a concerned look on their faces. A look that had been commonplace here for some time now. Marie Norton and Theodora stood at the top of the stairs waiting for me. When I saw the look on both of their faces, I understood what Apryl had meant. I yanked free from her grasp. Now it was my turn to knock her out of the way as I rushed up the stairs. I felt woozy when I reached the top.

Nathan wasn't awake when I arrived, but he no longer looked dead. There were changes happening. The final changes. His hair had lost its straw-like texture and was full, lush, and more colorful than before. Darker than the darkest black. Gone was the ashen look of his skin. It was still pale. The pink and peach hues of the living would never again be present in his complexion. I wanted to check one last thing, but I couldn't. I wouldn't. At least not until he woke up. Of course, once he woke up, there would be no more questions. It would be complete then, and we weren't far away from that now. I didn't know how long, but it didn't matter. Now I was going to sit here with him until that happened, and neither Master Thomas nor wild horses could drag me away from him. The queasiness that was rolling around inside me was something different, and I asked Marie to bring me a bucket or pot from the kitchen, just in case.

The sun set, and darkness flooded the room. Who was standing at the door, or just inside it, changed throughout the night. Amy came in and slept on my lap for a portion of the night, but she eventually left to go to my parents' bedroom to sleep comfortably. I never left. I didn't even stand up to stretch; that wasn't something I needed to do. What I needed to do was what I was doing. I held vigil over him, wanting to be the one there when he woke up. To be the first person he saw.

And, while I sat there, my mind rehearsed what I would say to him when he finally did. I went back and forth between throwing my arms around him, confessing my love, and crying, or apologizing and begging his forgiveness. I had to be careful. This was a moment he would remember forever. That first moment when he opens his eyes and experiences the world more vividly than he ever had before. The colors of the world are all brighter, like high definition on steroids. The sounds deeper and more complete. It's a full symphony with layer upon layer stacked up, exposing you to depths you never knew existed, where before, you were only hearing one instrument play the song of the universe, missing most of it.

For me, it was overwhelming at first. Everything flooded in on me all at once. Then the thirst, a burning down my throat, hit me like a freight train before I had a chance to absorb everything else. It was blindingly painful. Like the world's brightest spotlight shining right into my irises while the loudest concert blared into my ears. That was why the Nortons grabbed me and rushed me outside to hunt. There was no way I would have made it out there on my own. Nathan would go through the same once he woke, and he would need someone to help him, and that had to be me.

I watched over him for the rest of the next day, and the crowd at the door continued to rotate. Everyone stayed at the door, except the others like us. They all ventured in. Some checked on me, but all checked on him. I thought about this for a bit during one of the many moments of silence while I waited for him to rejoin us, and I had a theory of why this was. The others didn't understand what was happening to Nathan, and their distance was a show of either respect or possibly fear. For the rest of us, it was personal. We had all gone through it; we understood it better than anyone.

"If you want a break, I can watch him," offered Apryl. She sat on the other side of the bed from me. Nathan's body jerked. I jumped and grabbed both of his hands with mine. They were still limp.

"Sorry," Apryl apologized, and shifted again, causing Nathan to move.

"It's fine." I let go of one of Nathan's hands, but I kept a firm grip on the other, and laced my fingers with his.

"Why don't you take a little break?" Apryl offered again.

"I'm fine," I insisted.

"It could still be hours or days."

"I know."

"Can I point something out, just as a friend?" Apryl asked. There was a humorous, almost snarky tone to her voice.

"What?" I asked, curiously. I cut my eyes in her direction and saw her lean over closer to me.

"I know you want to be here when he first opens his eyes. I would too, but when was the last time you showered? Remember, senses are on edge when you wake." She smirked.

I sniffed at myself, but smelled nothing. That didn't mean I didn't stink. It had been a few days and the world around us had a way of adhering to us as we passed through it. Then I turned to check the mirror. Holy crap! I was the volcano of hot messes. Makeup streaks down my cheeks traced the path my tears had taken. Yep, all of the senses are razor sharp when a vampire first wakes. If this was the first image Nathan saw when he woke, he would run, and I wouldn't blame him.

"Go. I got him," Apryl said, and I rushed out of the room, happy no one was standing at the door to hear our conversation.

I took the quickest and hottest shower in the history of showers. I wanted the heat to melt away the grime and the pain of the last few days. It took the grime, but left the pain. All of that still existed, and it would for who knew how long. It would persist even after Nathan woke. It might even be stronger. Seeing him in his new form would be a potent reminder of what all had happened.

When I returned to my room, Amy was at the door, and Apryl was still on the bed. I asked Amy if she wanted to help me with my makeup. Magic wasn't going to work for me this time. Not that I couldn't use it easily. I could, and if I did, what Nathan would see would be better than any make-up artist could ever do, but there was something about it that felt fake, and I didn't want to be that. I wanted to be real.

After a few minutes of trying, I felt I had made a mistake. What I had applied so far made me look like a clown. Amy had managed to at least apply some blush to my cheek and blend it out correctly. She, at her young age, had more of a skill at this than I did, and that was surprising. I saw Apryl snickering behind in the mirror and shot her a harsh glance. She stood up and walked up behind me.

"Let me give you a hand."

I looked up at her and snipped back, "Since when have you become a make-up expert?" I both felt and heard the thump on the back of my head.

"We can't use this old stuff," she said, looking down at the contents of powder-based cosmetics I had Laura retrieve from my mother's dresser the night of the holiday ball. "Be right back," she disappeared in a flash, but returned just as fast, carrying her own bag. Her hands rummaged around in it, pulling out two vials of some flesh-colored liquids, a single compact of powder, and a single tube of lipstick. I knew what to do with that. It was basically all I had ever used when I was with the Nortons, and before that, my mother permitted me to use a little blush and light lipstick. That same blush was what I was trying to apply on my own, but obviously had forgotten how over the years. The lipstick, pink chiffon was the shade, was now nothing more than a solid stick of dried up color.

"Hold still." She grabbed my head and began tilting it back and forth to give her the best angles. I now knew what a mannequin felt like. I must have made a few faces or something while Apryl worked. Amy giggled a couple of times. I couldn't really see what she was doing. As soon as I could glance at the mirror, she was turning my head again.

"There," she announced as she backed away from me and admired her own work in the mirror. I looked and Amy climbed up in my lap to look at me in the mirror, too. It was going to hurt to do this, but I had to give it to Apryl. She knew what she was doing. I looked great. Actually, I looked better than great. I was radiant. If you ignored my eyes. They sat like lifeless islands in the middle of paradise.

"Wow," I said, and spun around, looking at Apryl.

She wiggled her fingers in the air. "See, you aren't the only one with magic in your fingers. It helps that I was a teen in this century before. I learned everything I needed to know from the mall make-up counters."

I reached up and ran my hands through wet and stringy hair. It was a mess and needed to be done. I grabbed a brush, and turned back to the mirror, but a movement, really the movement of a shadow behind on the wall behind Apryl grabbed my attention. One hand pushed her aside, while another did a quick brush through my hair, drying it and styling it into a wavy red frame around the work of art Apryl had just completed.

5

One would think a fanfare of trumpets would announce a person's rebirth. Maybe it should also be followed by symphonies and a choral hallelujah. Maybe that was what it was for those that were not cursed beings. For us, it's a silent awakening, with your eyes popping open first, then the flood of colors, smells, and sounds more vibrant than you ever remembered. Your senses are so sensitive to the world around you; nothing escapes your notice. If that sounds overwhelming? It is.

"Apryl, get Amy out of here!" Apryl had already thought of it and had her in her arms and out the door before I finished my command.

You hear everything. The wind, the creaking of the wood in the bed you are lying in as you first move, the movement of a creature over a mile away in the woods, and the rhythmic thumping of the heart in that same creature. What quickly becomes obvious are two realizations. That thumping is the more succulent sound you have ever heard. You want it, and you need it. You would run through a wall to get to it. The second observation is that there is one thumping missing from the world, and that is your own.

I quickly threw up a block to keep anyone from hearing or sensing the life growing inside me.

Nathan hadn't opened his eyes yet, but his hand moved, and his body jerked in the bed. I jumped from my chair to the bed, landing lightly to not jostle him. I grabbed his hand. At first, he stayed limp in my grasp, like he had the entirety of the last few days, but then his fingers curled and gripped mine, and I moved up higher on the bed, to be right next to his face. There was a twitching behind his eyelids. He was becoming aware of the world, and eventually they would spring open.

Mike, Clay, and Brad stood at the door with Jen and Kevin Bolden behind them. Kevin pushed through the crowd and walked in, but stayed a few steps from the bed.

"Larissa, we're here. Are you sure you're ready?"

"Do I have a choice?" Who knew if I was ready. It wasn't like I really had a choice in this matter. It was going to happen no matter what, and I didn't want to wait any longer for it. I wanted my Nathan back. I longed to hear his voice and to see that smile again. I did question if I would ever see it again once he found out what happened to him, and that was devastating to all of us. The world was a better place when he smiled, and god I needed to see it.

I also knew Kevin wasn't just asking if I was emotionally ready for this. He was talking more about the physical. He had more experience with newborns than anyone else I knew. He knew what we were in for and that was why he pushed past the others, and was in here with me. It was also why Clay and Brad made their first appearance up here. They were his backup.

"Martin took the others out of the house. It's just us."

Nathan's fingers gripped my hand firmer than before. There was life in them. I wrapped my other hand around our joined hands and rubbed his to tell him I was there. His fingers rubbed back. His thumb, doing the simple up and down as he often did when we held hands. I moved up closer to his head, about to leap out of my body and into his to drag him out of there when his head moved. It was just a simple roll to one side, but it was movement, and even Kevin Bolden moved closer in response.

His head rolled back, and then it happened. It wasn't slow. It was a spring-loaded surprise, exposing two black orbs that searched all around, trying to absorb as much of the world, the true world, that he could. The sight of them broke what was left of my heart. They were cold and emotionless. Not the pools of blue I often lost myself in the warmth and safety of. Those days were gone. That didn't stop the flood of other emotions to appear as tears, and my throwing myself across his chest, wrapping my arms around him.

Nathan's arms wrapped around me, reluctantly at first, and then he squeezed me closer, and his hands rubbed my back. His head bent forward, and he buried his face into the crook of my neck.

"It happened again, didn't it?" he asked, muffled.

"Umm huh," was all I could say.

"How many days this time?"

He didn't know. He absolutely didn't know. I looked up at Kevin and begged for help. How could Nathan not know what happened? He felt it all, but wait, that meant he felt it all before when we brought him back with the charm. Oh, my god. That is what he thinks happened again. That devastated me. Someone was going to have to tell him the truth, and it had to be me.

"Nathan," started Kevin, but I shook my head to wave him off. Nathan released his embrace, and I sat up a little and looked down at his tormented face. It appeared the realization of what had happened was settling in. Maybe his memories were all crashing in on him. I felt his body tense up underneath me.

"Larissa, you might want to move," warned Kevin. He inched forward defensively.

Nathan's hands gripped frantically at his throat. Kevin reached down for Nathan, but he threw his hand away. He then threw me off the bed and exploded toward the door. Clay and Mike had a grip on him, but both struggled to hang on. He was stronger than them at the moment. He was stronger than any of us at the moment. I was quickly up on my feet, ready to throw spells. Before I even realized what I was considering doing to my boyfriend. Kevin waved me off.

"Nathan, let us help you. You need to feed."

His head jerked back and looked at Kevin, and then at me. My boyfriend was gone, and there was an animal in his body. An uncaring, absent of love, harsh killing machine. Gone was the best of him, and the worst of me had replaced it.

Kevin grabbed him from behind and helped the others force Nathan out of the bedroom door. I heard several loud bangs and rushed out to the second-floor landing. At the bottom of the stairs was a pile of tangled bodies. Nathan was alreadt up on his feet and out the front door.

"I got him," yelled Clay, and he sped off.

"I hope so," Mike moaned as he stood and followed, a little slower.

Kevin looked up at me and before he followed, he said, "We will take good care of him."

Jen came up and put her arm around me on one side. Pam on the other. "Trust Kevin, he knows what he is doing."

It wasn't that I didn't trust him. That wasn't what was gnawing at me. It was guilt. Nathan was in this state because of me. I needed to be part of this and pulled away from them. Theodora caught my hand and pulled me back before I hit the top of the stairs.

"Larissa," she started, and then stopped. Tears flowed down my cheeks when our eyes locked. Theodora lowered her eyes and released my hand. She didn't say another word.

Marie Norton stood next to her, and I expected her to stop me like the others, but when I searched her for her objection, she mouthed, "Go." That is what I did. I took off down the stairs and out through the field, staying away from the rogue witch encampment and ran toward the shadows and what remained of St. Claire's coven.

The vampires weren't visible until I reached the trees, which took me an embarrassing long time to reach. I wasn't winded; that wasn't possible. I just wasn't as fleet of foot as I remembered. I was now slow for a vampire.

In the trees, Jean's followers, make that Jean's former followers, stood on either side lining a path that I had to assume the others had traveled. There were no footprints to follow or any broken branches. We were too graceful to leave either when we were on the move. Like ghosts moving through the world. I glanced back, just to check my own, and felt relieved there were no footprints or signs I had traveled in through that way. I had to check. I didn't feel myself in so many ways.

When I ran out of vampires lining the way, I had to trust my instincts to lead the way. Nathan was out here for one only one reason, and I followed its scent deeper into the dense woods and then turned south along the river. I came across Brad and Mike standing by a tree. They grabbed me as soon as I stepped past them.

"Let Mr. Bolden handle him," Mike said as he yanked me backward by the arm.

I yanked my arm free and took a few steps forward. Mike made another attempt to grab my arm, but all he got was air and a perturbed look.

"Where is he?"

Brad stepped forward and leaned over close to me. I dodged him, thinking he was going to grab me and yank me backwards. He stood back, holding both hands up in front of him until my glare relaxed. Then he pointed off in the distance, and I let my glare follow. I saw them. Mr. Bolden stood over Nathan while he sat on the ground. He braced his arms on his knees with his head drooped between them.

"What are they doing?" I whispered.

"Do you remember what happened after you fed for the first time?"

I did. The burning went away, and I felt renewed in a way I had never felt before. Then it hit me, "Oh," I muttered. The memory of that moment choked off the sound. That same feeling swept over me again and sent me trembling.

"Yep, that." Brad reached over and rubbed my shoulders, and I leaned into him. "Nathan will be okay. This is just something we all go through."

He was right, but that didn't make it any less heartbreaking, and knowing what he was feeling made me want to be there with him. I wanted to hold him, but I knew that wouldn't help him. This wasn't a time to tell someone that it would be okay and try to hug the pain away, and unfortunately, that was all I could offer at the moment. I remembered how I felt, but I couldn't remember how Marie and Thomas got me through it. I was sure it wasn't by holding me. I am sure they did at some point, but there was a speech, and a lot of talking, and that appeared to be what Mr. Bolden was doing now.

Nathan appeared to be listening, but he didn't appear to be hearing what Mr. Bolden was saying. There was an internal fight going on in his head that I was well aware of. When he sprang up to his feet, Mr. Bolden tried to calm him down, and cut off his attempts to leave, but then he missed, and Nathan stormed by. I stepped out away from Brad, right in Nathan's path. Nerves stirred inside me, and the urge to empty my stomach emerged again. I fought and pushed it back down, and steadied myself as Nathan approached. The look that greeted me was cold, and it had nothing to do with his now lifeless black eyes. There was no expression of recognition, just a stare that went through me. I took a step closer to his path, but Nathan walked right past me.

"Give him time." Mr. Bolden put his arm around me and gave me a half hug. He didn't appear concerned. "He has a lot to absorb. It will take time and soon the old Nathan will return. Everyone does."

He let go of me and followed behind Nathan. Mike fell in line behind him. Brad waited for me to join him, and we walked out of the woods together, with a stewing Nathan leading the way.

"Just give him–" started Brad.

"I know... time." I finished for him.

He shrugged. "It's hard. You remember that don't you?"

"I guess." My answer drew a question filled look from Brad. I had a feeling I was missing something, but I didn't ask. I sped up, and Brad tried to grab my hand, but caught nothing but air.

Mike made the same attempt as I passed him, and missed.

Mr. Bolden didn't grab me, but he whispered a warning, "Larissa, don't." I ignored it.

"Nathan," I called out to him and reached for his shoulder. My hand was about to touch him when he spun around. The frigid expression I had seen in the woods was gone, and I would have given anything for it to return. It would have been a thousand times better than the anger-fueled look that had replaced it.

Nathan spun around and seethed, "Don't." Then his eyes remained locked on mine. The emotion-filled windows to his soul were closed. Around them, his face steamed and stewed, fueled by rage and pain. I wanted to remove it. I wanted to pull that weight from him, but I couldn't, and with how he looked at me, he didn't even want me to try.

He left me standing there at the bottom step of the porch. I just watched as he walked in through the front door. Mr. Bolden passed with a simple pat on the shoulder. Brad passed by with nothing, but Mike muttered, "We tried to warn you." That earned him a punch to his stomach as his reward. Brad snickered.

Once inside, I looked around for Nathan, but he was no longer in the front entry. I checked the parlor, but found nothing. Theodora walked down the hall toward me and rounded around the newel post and glided up the stairs gracefully.

"He's up here, but give me a minute. Some things require a woman's touch."

I watched as she ascended and disappeared into my bedroom. That woman, so graceful, so beautiful, and so alone with my boyfriend. My foot was on the bottom stair before I knew it and I was at the top in a dash, but something stopped me at the doorway. I stood there and watched.

Theodora sat next to him on the bed. Her legs crossed, with one ankle behind the other. She leaned into Nathan as she spoke. A hand occasionally touched him on the leg. Each touch was light, and from my vantage point, slightly seductive. Light and delicate. It lingered in an area before being removed, only to return to a new location. They returned a little too often for my liking. Nathan's eyes appeared to study her. Her shape, her lips. I had to shake that thought from my head. She was not flirting with my boyfriend, and he wasn't flirting with her. I told myself that repeatedly, but I couldn't miss the fact that he was sitting there, seemingly enjoying her non-flirting a bit too much. I had to stop my mind from running off in that direction. Jealousy wasn't a feeling I was familiar with, and so far, I didn't like it.

The two of them spoke softly. Her tone was sweet and smooth. Whatever she was saying, which I couldn't hear, was being well received. Nathan's face had relaxed. The anger and ferocity that had been present had melted away moments after I arrived at the door. He looked more like himself, and he even interacted with her. Was he asking her questions? What were the questions? There I was, feeling jealous again. I wanted to be the one he went to. Who was she to take my role? I wanted to walk in there and assert myself and take my rightful place, but then another voice spoke to me. It was logic, and I rarely heard it over my emotions. This time, it was as loud and clear as a cannon shot. Theodora was hundreds of years my senior. She knew more and had experienced more than I had. She had seen this probably dozens, if not hundreds, of times. She was the oldest, and best prepared of all of us.

After a conversation that lasted long into the afternoon, Theodora gave Nathan a hug and then stood up and took her exit of the room. I couldn't help but notice how Nathan's eyes traced her body as she walked away from him. That was something I filed away for later. There were bigger concerns now. At least that was what that logical voice that still had control of my being said. She closed the door behind herself, and I held out a hand to hold the door open. I was going in now, or was, until she looked at me with her big eyes and pursed full lips and shook her head. I dropped my protest and stood there face to face with a closed wooden door.

"Give him some... time."

My mind completed the statement before Theodora had a chance.

"He is dealing with so much. Sadness. Anger. Name any negative emotion and that is what is going on inside of him at the moment. It will just take time."

"The first kill is always the hardest," I agreed.

She laughed. "Oh child, you think this is what that is all about?"

I nodded, believing that was all it could be, but she shook her head.

"He knows what he is, and as a result he realizes what had happened, and what it means for everything. To most, that is a frightening and depressing realization. The life they knew is gone in so many ways. You remember that moment, don't you?"

I didn't. I didn't at all. When I woke up, I didn't remember my life before. Being what I was at that moment was all I remembered. My life before, was a big black hole. She walked me downstairs and explained more, and I finally asked her what she told him. She said she told him about what she felt, which she still remembered as clearly as if it had happened just yesterday, and explained that everything he felt was natural. Then she told me what she always tells new vampires in this situation. It's a statement that slapped most of them right across the face. That everything they felt was wrong. Life is not over; it is just the beginning. Your life can be as much like your old life as you want it. It's completely up to you to make what you want out of it. She had one last point that I remembered hearing her tell me clearly on one of my visits. We are beautiful creatures and should live life to the fullest.

Theodora left me on the front porch. She needed to head back to her place for a bit to attend to her "human" business, but promised to come back tomorrow or tomorrow night to check in. The last thing she said to me before she hugged me and bid her farewell was an instruction that I felt would be impossible to fulfill. I wasn't to go to Nathan. He would come to me when he was ready. I wasn't sure if she truly understood what she was asking of me, but she was rather insistent and made me promise.

So, I sat out on the porch and waited. I fought every urge I had to run up the stairs to him. Twice I was weak and made it as far as the front door before I stopped and returned to my perch in the rocking chair. When darkness fell, the others returned home from their visit with the rogue witches. Amy seemed to think it was some kind of fair and talked about all the magic tricks she saw. Stan bragged about a few of her own tricks, remarking to me she was rather advanced for a shifter of that age. She sat with me until she dozed off and then Lisa grabbed her and took her in with her to get some sleep. Martin, Rob, and Dan stood out on the porch for a few minutes, just staring out at the sight before them. A large camp of witches on one side, and dozens of vampires hovering in the trees on the other.

"I don't really see a need for us to do a patrol, do you?" Martin asked. I agreed and sent the three of them inside.

Throughout the night, random vampires emerged from the house and attempted to make small talk. It didn't take any of them long before they realized I wasn't really in the mood for it, and they either sat there in silence or went back inside. I wanted and needed the solitude to ponder what Nathan was going through. The emotions, not from all he sensed in this new world, but from what he felt he had lost. I didn't have a reference point for that, at least not personally. I remembered the story Clay had told of those first few days. It sounded like he was a tormented soul until we, I mean the Boldens, found him. Was that how Nathan felt? I sure hope not, but feared he did.

Out among the woods, vampires mingled and as darkness set in and the witches' camp quieted. Groups upon groups mingled with one another. Some came as close as the line that used to be made of runes, just to look around before retreating to the shadows. The line had faded significantly, losing both its luster and strength throughout the day. I hadn't redrawn the line, so nothing stopped them from coming over, except choice. They were choosing not to, or that was what it seemed. Mostly, they appeared unable to make a choice. They have spent years, decades, or centuries doing what Jean commanded. Now they were on their own, and that seemed to be unsettling for them. I felt a brief moment of responsibility there and decided to talk to Theodora about it when she returned to see if anything could be done.

An hour after the witching hour, which really had nothing to do with witches except for the fact that they were all asleep at that moment, the door creaked behind me. Laura and Pam were on the swing, and out of the corner of my eye I saw both of their heads shoot toward the door before they stood up and walked inside.

"So, you and I have something in common," said a familiar voice behind me.

Tears came to my eyes at hearing his voice. "What's that?" I said, playing along, forcing my voice to sound stronger than it was at the moment.

"We have both turned twice."

"Sucks doesn't it?"

"Yep." Then he placed a hand on my shoulder briefly before he leaned down and hugged my neck.

6

He sat in the chair beside me for a long time. There was silence between us, but there wasn't distance. Which was something I worried would be there. It seemed, as absurd as it might sound to say, normal. None of the speeches I rehearsed in my head for the moment he woke up made it out. They didn't seem important anymore. The one where I apologized and begged his forgiveness seemed limp and worthless for what had happened, but at the same time, it didn't appear needed anymore. Nathan never regarded me with a look that had an appearance of hatred or blame. The one where I threw myself across him and confessed my love didn't seem to be needed either. We weren't sitting on top of each other, and hadn't shared a great embrace, but there didn't seem to need to be one. Him sitting here, with the little looks in my direction from time to time, told me everything I needed. That we, at least for the moment, were okay. That didn't stop my heart from breaking every time I saw those black eyes. We might be okay, but I wasn't so sure I was.

We sat and looked at the scene that used to be my front yard. There were still scars on the ground from the fight that occurred a few days ago. They were something I could easily fix, but hadn't. I really hadn't even looked at them before now. The shadows created by the moonlight made the indentation where I slammed Jean St. Claire down into the ground appear enormous, where in reality it was only a dent of a few inches in the ground. Looking at it now didn't bring any of the pride like I had felt before. All I felt was the painful reminder of what had happened, and how I didn't stop it.

"Witches, I assume?" asked Nathan, breaking the silence.

"Rogue witches."

He looked over at me and asked, "What?"

"Rogue witches. Ones that are exiled by the council, or disagree with the council," I explained, looking out at the camp. My mind wondered how many there were, and how many witches there were in the world? I didn't think there would be all that many, but this camp was huge, and those were just the rogue witches that were in the area.

"I thought they called those Larissa," sniped Nathan, completely deadpanning the shot while looking forward.

"That is a special level of hell. These witches haven't achieved that yet." I fired back. "It's between this and the prison." I nodded out to the camp of roque witches.

"Prison?" Nathan asked. He leaned forward in his chair and looked at me with a cockeyed expression. He thought I was kidding. Oh, contraire.

"Yes, there is a prison for the most dangerous witches. I just found out about it." It was true. Marcus Meridian told me about it. Which made me wonder why the council threatened his family with the removal of their magical power instead of just being put in prison where they couldn't do any harm to the council. Marcus told me it was to send a message to anyone that might support them. The fear of being stripped themselves would keep them from doing anything that the council might feel was a threat.

"It's a horrible place, underground in a deep cavern on an island that no one knows is there, in a place you can't find."

"Of course it is," he said, and winked.

"No, I'm serious. The sun never rises, and it always rains. Underground there are bottomless pits and rivers of lava. Anyone sent there is there for life. There is no parole, and the council is judge and jury." I looked at him as seriously as I could and his own expression changed as he sat back in his chair. I made note of how straight he sat. It was very un-Nathan like. "Yep, it's pretty much a bad place."

"And they call us savage," remarked Theodora from behind us. I turned around, but not as fast as Nathan did. His grin was expansive. I didn't remember her returning, but perhaps I was so stuck in my own thoughts she glided right by me. "I hope we aren't interrupting anything." She stepped out the door. Marie Norton followed.

"Oh, no. You aren't interrupting anything at all," Nathan was quick to say, and his eagerness ruffled me slightly, but I held my tongue, which was very un-Larissa like.

"We were thinking it might be time to go out and meet your cousins," Theodora said with a smile.

"Sounds good." Nathan stood up, again a little too quickly. This would be what I would call the Theodora effect, and I would pick an appropriate time to correct it with an equal and opposite reaction, but that time was not now.

She led the way off the porch, and Nathan wasn't far behind her. I watched, annoyed, and then turned to Marie. A realization of what we were doing had set in, and I didn't agree. I grabbed the woman I had regarded so long as my mother by the hand and yanked her close. "Mom," I caught myself, and there was an awkward glance between us. I knew this moment was bound to happen eventually, and again; this would be something we would have to settle later. I had other concerns that were at the forefront of my mind that needed tending to. "Is this a good idea?"

Marie reached over and brushed a lock of hair away from my face. Her touch brought back so many memories of all the years we pretended to be mother and daughter. Wait, I take that back. No one was pretending. This was complicated, and it was complicating what I was trying to get through.

"It is," she answered calmly. "Theodora and I talked about it, and we both agree it would be good for Nathan to meet others like us. Others that from all appearances are just normal people living normal lives, even with what they are."

"But this soon?" I asked urgently. Nathan had just come back from it, and like Theodora told me earlier, he was dealing with a ton of emotions. "This isn't too soon?"

"It's exactly the right time. Now come on." She wrapped both hands around mine and led me off the porch. We had walked this way many times together in our backyard, back in Virginia. Usually headed out to the shed where Thomas was working on the furniture and cabinets he built for others. It felt natural and good, but odd, all at the same time. We were in the wrong place.

Marie giggled just before she let go of my hand. "Go reclaim your boyfriend."

She gave me a big shove forward, and I reached him in just a few steps. I grabbed his hand. Our fingers interlaced together perfect, like they had so many times. Now the warmth I always enjoyed was missing. I felt something cold come over me as several shadows emerged out of the woods as we approached the tree line.

"Marie?" cried a thick creole female voice. With it, I felt the glare of dozens of sets of eyes. My body tensed up. Mr. Helms had taught me well.

"Oh God, it is you," cried the voice again, and then out of the darkness ran a middle-aged blonde woman in a simple navy-blue dress that went to her knees, she wore brown leather boots which were caked with mud from the field. "It is you," she repeated.

When she was close enough for us to see the attractive features of her face, Marie ran to meet her with a cry of, "Frances!"

The two women hugged, slinging each other around one another as they spun and shrieked. A small group of vampires splintered off from the others beyond the tree line and joined the two women. There were hugs and warm embraces all around. A man grabbed Marie by the face, looking at her with what appeared to be tears in his eyes, and then bent down and kissed her on both cheeks.

Nathan and I watched the sight of Marie's old friends welcoming her home. We heard greeting after greeting with a few adding in, "We thought you were dead." It would appear no one in this crowd knew Jean St. Claire had her locked in that dark dungeon being tortured. With how they greeted her, I wondered if they had known, would they have stood up to him to do something about it?

The joyful reunion turned solemn when I heard someone ask about Thomas, and Marie's head bowed as she told them. She didn't hesitate to tell them what happened and who was behind it. Several of them turned and looked away from her as she identified the assailant that took his life. Others showed anger, with one pounding his fist into the palm of his hand. "You should have reached out to us," he exclaimed. Marie just ignored him, and tried to turn the conversation away from such a dark topic. Her next topic was, well, me.

Marie turned and motioned for Nathan and I to join her. "Everyone, this is Larissa Dubois, and…" there was a collective gasp following my name that drowned out Nathan's introduction. A few stepped back, while the others stepped forward with curiosity.

"So, this is her?" asked the same man that pounded his fist at hearing who was behind Thomas' death.

"Yes," responded Marie, then she turned and introduced her passionate friend. "Larissa, this is Fred Harvey. A dear old friend of mine and your father's… I mean Thomas'." Hearing the term father caused several odd looks and Marie waved an embarrassed hand in the air before delicately placing it just below her collarbone. Something I had seen her do many times in the past.

The tall, redheaded man with a long red beard that hung down over the vest of the suit he wore, which appeared to be several centuries out of date, stepped forward and looked me over. "You're still a witch?"

I figured the best way to answer that, and any other questions the others may have, was to show them instead of telling them. I pulled my hand away from Nathan's grasp and held both hands up in front of me. A glowing green orb appeared between them, then green flames shot from it, illuminating everyone. But I wasn't done yet. The flames swirled as I played with the strings of the surrounding universe. I allowed them to climb high into the sky, carrying the orb with it at breathtaking speed. Then a single bolt of lightning cracked across the clear sky. I held both hands up as if to say, "Anymore questions."

"She's her father's daughter," proclaimed Theodora. "Just as powerful, if not more so than Maxwell ever was."

"Well, that explains everything I guess," muttered Fred Harvey.

"Yes, it does," said the woman who first greeted Marie. The woman looked at me through the tears that had formed in her eyes. Her bottom lip quivered.

I knew her name was Frances from hearing her and Marie greet each other, but there was something familiar about her. I first saw it when my little light show chased the shadows away from her face. She walked forward and reached for both of my hands, and I held them out instinctively. Her face was familiar, and my mind raced to place it. It wouldn't have been odd if I have had seen many of these people around town, but this was more than just a casual acquaintance or a one time passing on the street. Then my mind moved her blond hair up into a bun on the back of her head, and her full name escaped in a single phrase, "Frances Rundle."

"You remembered," she beamed. "My, you grew up to be the spitting image of your mother."

Then my mind exploded with memories. Frances Rundle was the woman that attempted, albeit a failed attempt, to teach me to play piano for two years. It was all my mother's idea. An outlet that wasn't magic related. The problem was, I had a tin ear and wasn't particularly good. That's not exactly accurate. I was horrible, unless I used magic, which I never did when she was present. It was the strict rule in our house. No magic around visitors unless my parents told me they were witches, which they never told me if Frances Rundle was or not. They most certainly didn't tell me she was a vampire, and I had to wonder if she was at that time or not. This wasn't a question I knew how to ask.

Frances pulled me in and hugged me, and it felt like it always did before, all those years ago. "It's so great to see you," I said. She let go and backed away, beaming as she looked back at me several times.

Nathan leaned over and asked, "Who's that?"

"My piano teacher," I said.

"I didn't know you played."

"I don't. I stunk at it," I confessed to Nathan.

"You just never put in the practice time," said Frances as she settled back in with the group.

Dang, that vampire hearing.

The man who first approached Marie and kissed her on both cheeks walked forward, and I prepared for another introduction by searching his face for any familiarity. There was none. Not even the hint of anyone I used to know or may have seen once or twice, and much to my surprise, he didn't approach me. He approached Nathan with an outstretched hand. The man was tall and slender, a good two inches taller than Nathan, which meant he was a giant to me. His deep voice completed the picture.

I nudged Nathan, who seemed to be leery of the outstretched hand. He reached out slowly, eventually taking the man's hand. "You must be the young man that we saw Jean bite. I want to say seeing you rush and tackle him away from her," he glanced in my direction, "was one of the bravest acts I have ever seen."

It was one of the stupidest I had ever seen, and he had now done it twice, but I wasn't about to say that aloud and ruin Nathan's moment. I just stood there and smiled.

"Thanks," said Nathan reluctantly.

"I guess I should also welcome you. It will take a bit, but you will soon forget anything happened." The man let Nathan's hand go, but added. "We are all here to help."

"Thank you, sir," responded Nathan.

"Sylvester's the name. Sylvester Webb."

Theodora put her arm around Nathan and said, "Sylvester is a good person to know. He is over eight hundred years old. He knows more about blending in with human society than anyone I know."

"Three continents," he stated proudly. "I've even fought in every major war, including... the French Revolution." He threw the last bit out with a convincing French accent.

"I need to borrow these two for a moment. I promised to bring them back," announced Theodora. "I want them to meet *him*." She turned Nathan easily with the lightest of touches, and I grabbed his hand to remind him I was there.

"Nathan, everyone you just met lives in New Orleans and has rather normal lives. If you didn't already know they were vampires, would you have known?" she asked.

"Not really."

"That is something I want you to remember. We live how we want. The only difference is we don't have some of the same limitations humans do," she said as we walked deeper into the woods, passing small groupings of vampires as we went.

"You make it sound so simple."

"I agree," I interjected into their seemingly private conversation. It did sound simple, too simple.

"It is," she insisted. "It's our mind that complicates things. As soon as you free your mind to the possibilities that life brings, how simple it really is reveals itself." Theodora continued to prance proudly forward into the woods, not that she ever gave the impression she was anything but proud. This woman exuded confidence.

I looked back at Marie, who was a few steps behind us. She mouthed, "she's right." Huh. Leave it to my brain to not see it. Of course, that didn't really surprise me. The girl that over thinks everything. Simple doesn't have a chance in my world.

"Marteggo," called Theodora. She stopped dead in her tracks and went down to a single knee. Marie Norton stepped up next to me and did the same.

I followed suit and yanked Nathan down to give him the hint. I bowed my head, but then looked up slightly to see what all this was about. There were two males, dressed in the black suits and slicked back hair like what Reginald and the rest of Jean's most loyal followers wore, but they weren't the only people here. There was someone else, and he was different, very different. He sat on the roots of a grand mangrove tree, sprawled out as if it were his throne. His posture had a little slump to it, and long, black, curly locks hung down around his face and across his broad shoulders. He even dressed differently from the others. He wore boots, and jeans, and a white shirt that almost looked like a t-shirt.

"Theodora," his voice returned. "It's been a while."

Theodora stood up, and I waited for Marie to do the same before I joined them.

"I could say the same for you. We haven't seen you around these parts in what, two hundred years?"

"I didn't like the neighborhood," he grumbled back.

"Who is he?" I whispered to Marie.

"Better question, who are you?" he asked, pointing a gnarly finger in my direction.

"Marteggo, let me introduce you to the vampire that forced Jean to leave this area. This is Larissa Dubois." Theodora reached back and yanked my hand free from Nathan's, and pulled me forward toward the man that now looked more beast than man sitting there in shadows. "Larissa, this is Marteggo Dupoint."

She introduced him as if I should know who he was.

"I guess I should thank you for ridding us of that fungus, but he isn't gone, only displaced. So, I will hold it for now." He leaned down from the mangrove roots. "He will be back. Mark my words. He is after something, and has been for years. Something very dangerous."

"She's the witch," spouted Theodora.

Marteggo leaped down off the root and stomped toward me, emerging out of the shadows and crossing through several beams of moonlight, giving clarity to who we were speaking with. This was no beast; this was a man. A large burly man, with long curly black hair that flowed behind him in the wind as he walked. His face, like Nathan's, had chiseled features, or at least what I could see did. A jet-black beard covered his mouth. Nothing hid his black eyes, which appeared to have a permanent scowl. "You? You're, the witch?"

From beside me, Theodora clarified. "She is the daughter of Maxwell Dubois. Didn't you recognize the name?"

He threw his head back as far as it would go and laughed a bellowing laugh that echoed through the woods. His clear charm dangled on a long gold chain and glistened in the moonlight. His two escorts didn't join in. Theodora covered her mouth, hiding what appeared to be a smirk of her own.

"I call that a huge and well-deserved dose of karma. Too bad it wasn't laced with some poison." he said. "You have brought me some great news, my sweets." He grabbed Theodora by the waist and spun her around. The rough exterior he had dropped away as she wrapped her arms around him. I looked at Nathan to be sure he was seeing this. Not that Theodora threatened me, but I couldn't ignore how beautiful she was. With how Marteggo Dupoint devoured her, he saw her that way too.

He dropped her to her feet, but still held on to her. She plastered herself to his side. "Now, Miss Dubois. Don't for a second believe this is the last you will hear from him. The man is not well, and you have now wounded him, yet again." Marteggo warned with a wag of a finger. "First you deprived him of what he wanted, then you defeated him, and probably worst of all, you took his world from him. That won't go unpunished."

I wanted to thank him for pointing out the obvious, but against my nature, I held my tongue. I still didn't know who this man was. All I knew was he appeared different from the others, and Theodora seemed to trust him. I needed more information before I did as well.

"And who is this big strapping boy?" He slapped Nathan on the arm and almost knocked him to the ground.

"This is her boyfriend, Nathan Saxon. He saved Larissa from Jean, tackling him to give her the opening she needed," introduced Theodora.

"Well, any enemy of Jean's is a friend of mine." He reached out, shook Nathan's hand. "A brave move. We need more like you that will step up–"

"He was human when he did it," interrupted Theodora, stopping Marteggo mid-statement.

He looked at Nathan, shocked, and ripped his hand back. "Son, were you stupid? Didn't you know who you were attacking and what would happen?"

Nathan appeared mortified standing there and stammered, trying to answer.

"Relax son. It's okay. I say we need a little more stupid and reckless abandon these days." Marteggo slapped him again. "It's great to meet you."

My inner voice escaped and asked, "But who are you?"

"Well," Marteggo straightened himself up, and tugged at his shirt. "Marteggo Dupoint at your service."

"I know your name, but who are you?" I asked, feeling there was more to this man, and why Theodora brought us to see him.

"Well, maybe I should take that question," interjected Theodora. "This will sound like some fantasy story, but it is all true."

I half wanted to say try me, considering the world I had seen over the last several months. There wasn't much I wouldn't believe anymore.

"Marteggo was a pirate that sailed the Gulf and Caribbean several hundred years ago. A vampire in Port-au-Prince bit him, and he became the legendary Vampire Pirate until he settled down here. Once word got out who he was, vampires flocked to him, and, well, he became the de facto leader here."

"Not something I wanted, mind you," interrupted Marteggo. "I wanted to find someone and suckle all that life had to offer. Not tell people how to live their lives."

"Which you never really did,"

Marteggo held up a finger to emphasize the point. "True. I didn't unless someone caused a problem. Then they stood before the mast."

Now I was confused. If I understood what Theodora had said, Marteggo was really the true leader of the New Orleans coven, and if that was true, what happened? Something had to have for Jean St. Claire to take control, or, and my head was swimming at this point, was there some kind of split, like in the world of witches? Why couldn't anything be simple?

"Then I have a question."

"Go ahead."

Marteggo righted himself and crossed his arms. He was an impressive image with a stature that demanded respect or created fear. I had a feeling either worked for him. The weight of his presence caused a hesitation on my part as I wondered if I should ask what I was curious about. "Then..." my voice cracked, but I cleared it quickly. "What happened? If you were the leader, how did Jean take over?"

The gregarious smile that had adorned Marteggo's face slipped away, and he backed away from Theodora. She attempted to hold on cautiously. Maybe that fleeting warning in my head was right. The giant man sank back into the darkness and sat on the edge of the mangrove roots he used as his throne when we arrived. There was a huff before he leaned forward against his tree trunk thighs.

"You already know Jean St. Claire, so you shouldn't have to ask that," he sneered, and glanced to the side before looking back with a pained expression. "But, since you asked, I will tell you. He was a sniffling whiner in our world. Always complaining, why do we need to act more human? Why do we need to hide? Why shouldn't we show how superior we are? Always this and that. Now, I will say, I never ruled. I refused to. I thought of what I did as leading by example, and yes, I hid what I was by blending into the world around me when I had to and avoided humans as often as I could. That is what we must do. Nothing would be gained by us showing the world our true colors, but fear, forcing us further into the shadows. Just like Theodora and many others have done. That shouldn't stop us from living the best life we can, and I wanted to enjoy life, not spend it trying to control and enslave."

Theodora smiled and nodded as he mentioned her.

"Jean was never satisfied with that, and did the only thing he could do. He couldn't physically challenge me." There was a deep chested chuckle.

"Few could," added Theodora.

"Thank you, my love. Jean knew it too, so he didn't. He did the only thing anyone like him could do. He fostered discontent in the masses. He found a few that felt as he had, and it grew. What is the saying? One bad apple ruins the barrel. He spread like a cancer through our community. Before I knew it, there were more of those than there were of us. There was no grand announcement. No election of sorts. Just a switch in the balance of power."

"Why didn't you fight back?" asked Nathan.

"Well now, that is an interesting question there, my boy. At first, we didn't. Remember, we just wanted a peaceful life, which is what you should strive for too." He wagged a finger toward the newest vampire of the bunch. "Heartache and pain comes with wanting more. There is nothing wrong with taking the best life this world offers. At first, we let him do as he wanted, and we watched. When he stepped too far and threatened to destroy that peace for all of us, there was no choice. We fought, we lost, and they hunted us until we gave up and left. It's why some of us are way back here, and not with the others out there. Distrust still runs deep, but hearing the news that someone forced Jean out, we had to come see for ourselves." Marteggo stood up and left his throne of roots. "Don't take my presence as a return to power. It's quite the opposite. I hope it is a return of the peace."

I hoped he was right too, but nothing at that moment felt like peace. It felt more chaotic than normal, and sitting out there threatening to pour more chaos on it was Jean. My mouth went off without a filter again to point out that fact. "Jean is still out there."

"It's Larissa, isn't it?" Marteggo asked.

I nodded.

"I know, and his absence might only be temporary, but it still gives a moment of peace and maybe enough will enjoy that. If enough do, it may dissolve any chance of him finding support when he returns."

I felt it coming, and I knew I needed to push it back down. It wasn't another bout of nausea. That would have been better. The pressure built up inside, and nothing was going to stem it. It needed to be said. Even while happiness and warmth appeared to return to our group. Marteggo embraced Theodora. Nathan put his arm around me and pulled me close. I should have just let it go, but I didn't. I shook off Nathan's arm and took a step forward, and let out the storm cloud that had bumbled up inside. They had to know.

"I think he has the support of the witches."

I looked around, expecting to find expressions of doom and gloom, but I heard laughter. First from Marteggo, and then from what I believe were his escorts that stood on either side of the mangrove.

"Good, let them deal with his ass," replied Marteggo. "If you ask me, they deserve him. They are no better than he is. Them and that council. Neither are happy with just being who they are. They all want more."

Theodora joined in with a reserved snicker. Even Marie giggled at the comment. Nathan and I were the only ones that didn't. I knew the truth. This wasn't just a relocation of the problem of Jean to someone else. This was taking two colossal problems and creating one gigantic issue, but I let it drop, at least for now. There was a part of me that believed this was more of a witch problem.

"You seem so serious. This is all good news." Marteggo let go of Theodora and came over, wrapping Nathan and I in the largest embrace I had ever felt. We were like dolls against his massive frame. "This is good news." His voice sounded muffled, with my head buried against his chest. "Come, let's drink and tell stories," he said as he released us both. Then he put a single hand on Nathan's chest. "Well, we drink, you don't. You are still much too young, but you can listen."

He walked around us, laughing as he continued out of the woods toward the other vampires. Theodora joined him and walked with him hand-in-hand. Marie fell in behind, and I found Nathan and I were the only two left, so we followed as well.

7

The first rays of morning were cutting through the openings in the canopy of branches overhead when we headed back up to the house. The night was great, and I had to swallow a little crow and admit that Theodora and Marie were right. Letting Nathan meet others like us helped. It helped him realize his life wasn't over. If anything, as many pointed out, the best parts of his life were ahead of him. I hoped I was part of that picture, not that I had a lot of reason to doubt it. Most of the night, Nathan held me in his arms as we listened to stories and gems of advice from those that had been vampires longer.

Mike, Jeremy, and Brad were out on the porch, horsing around when we arrived back at the farmhouse. I wanted to remind them there was a house full of others sleeping behind them, but every light except the parlor was off, so no one seemed to be bothered. The three of them straightened up as soon as they saw us approaching and stood at the rail grinning.

"Where have you kids been?" asked Mike. He stood right at the railing with his arms crossed, tapping his foot. Of course, being a vampire, it sounded like a woodpecker on speed.

"You could have called. We have been so worried." Brad said, struggling to keep a straight face.

"Oh, knock it off," cracked Pamela from behind them in the door. "They were the same place you guys were. Out there with the others, enjoying life."

The three of them turned and watched as we walked by. Mike grabbed Nathan by the shoulder and whispered something into his ear. I couldn't hear it, but I saw the grin grow on his face, and then felt him grip my hand and yank me through the door, almost trampling Pamela. "What the hell?" I asked, and I didn't get an answer.

We were one foot on the stairs when Nathan jerked to a stop. The grip on my hand tightened, and his head snapped. I was so used to what had his attention, I never really noticed it anymore unless I focused on it. The years of being like this had desensitized me. To a newborn, there was no ignoring it. Its presence overrode your thoughts. Your body just reacted to its presence, just like Nathan was now. I spun around on the stairs as he ran for the parlor. In there, Laura had sprung up from the settee and rushed to meet Nathan at the door. Amy, who had been sleeping soundly in her lap, was now startled awake. The first sounds of a scream left her mouth. I watched as he shoved Laura against the wall. Mike, Brad, and Jeremy rushed through the front door, but they would never catch him. He had a head start, and being a newborn was still faster and stronger.

My hand reached to grab him, but he was too far. That was when I squeezed the vibrations of the world and shoved them forward, knocking him facedown on the floor. He didn't lay there stunned as long as I had hoped. He jumped back up to his feet in an instant. I had one trick up my sleeve and pulled it out. He stopped and stood there, confused.

Amy crawled back behind the settee and screamed. Laura pulled herself along the floor to Amy. Each movement appeared pained, but that didn't stop her from reaching Amy and pulling her close. Nathan stood there, clueless. I had cast the spell so fast; I couldn't even remember what I had projected for him to see. This wasn't the simple trick I played at Theodora's making Master Thomas appear to be a vampire. That was my first choice, and albeit easiest, but I couldn't trust that Nathan would stop, even when the feeling disappeared if he could still see her. This way, there was no doubt. She wasn't there, and neither was he.

The scream had woken the entire house, and Rob and Martin bounded down the stairs. Steve joined them. I saw the concern on his face as soon as he took in the scene.

"She's okay. I have Nathan under control," I said, standing right next to Nathan, just in case I needed to intervene again. Steve pushed down the stairs the rest of the way and pushed through Mike's shoulder to get through the door. Mike hissed with the thud of the impact, and Steve growled. Martin and Rob took another step down the stairs, but backed off when Mike didn't follow Steve into the parlor. He made a beeline for Amy, who was in Laura's arms.

"She's safer with her own kind," he said with a coldness I hadn't seen in him before, but it was common from Ms. Parrish. Steve wasn't just making a suggestion. He reached down and yanked Amy from Laura's grasp. She went willingly and stopped screaming. She sniffed as they passed us. I reached out and stroked her head while she looked leerily at Nathan standing confused in the center of the room. Laura shot me a look of disdain that I couldn't explain at the moment. It was both pointed and targeted. There was no mistaking that.

I ushered Rob and Martin back up the stairs, not waiting to take any chances at all. As I expected, both protested, stating they could handle things themselves, but I urged them as nicely as I could to go back upstairs, not wanting a fight inside. They didn't listen. At least not to me. When Pam and Apryl both made the same suggestion, they reluctantly headed upstairs. I gave it a few seconds to be sure before I let Nathan return. His head jerked around, taking in the parlor, and probably wondering where what he saw went.

"What happened?" he asked.

"You tried to eat Amy," sniped Laura.

Nathan's jaw dropped and his hands reached out into the room for an explanation. He looked around the room, which was now all vampires. "I didn't."

"Oh, you did," responded Mike.

Apryl hit Mike with a sharp elbow. "She's okay, Nathan. You couldn't control yourself. It's not your fault at all," she explained.

He looked back at me, horrified and shaken. "How could I?"

"Nathan, darling." I reached up and caressed his cheek. "You couldn't help it. Things are too raw right now for you to stop yourself, but she is okay. I did a little." I waved my hand in front of his face. "You were someplace else and didn't even know she was here."

Nathan collapsed in the chair in the corner and held his head in his hands. "How could I?" He repeated, more mournful this time.

"Nathan, you will learn to control it. Trust us," Jeremy said.

I wanted him to look up. If he had, he would have seen an entire room of smiling vampires, and boy were we a sight, fangs and all.

Apryl walked over and kneeled down next to him. She looked around at each of us cautiously, and her attempt to be the peacemaker drew some odd looks from the room. Apryl would be the last person I would pick, but she was the one that stepped forward. Compassion and her were an odd couple. "Trust us, in time, you will learn how to handle it. We all have. Remember, back in the coven, we were all in the same classes, and I never once wanted to attack anyone."

"None of us did," added Mike.

"Well, except for Gwen," concluded Apryl. There were smirks and a few admonishing looks in her direction at that comment.

I had refrained from smirking and motioned for her to get up and took her spot next to my boyfriend. I reached up and pried a hand from his head. It still shook, as his mind tried to process what had happened. I thought of what Clay had told me about his encounter with his parents in those first two days after he turned. It was the same thing, and if he were here, maybe hearing about that could help get through to Nathan, but Clay, Marie, and the Boldens were still outside with the others. It was up to me, and to be honest, I wouldn't have it any other way.

"Nathan, she's safe. None of us would let anything happen to her. Trust us on that. In time, what you feel now will stop feeling like an uncontrollable raging fire, and turn into nothing but an itch that you can easily ignore, but... until then. I can help you like I did tonight. I can mask Amy and the others."

"Can you?" he asked through his remaining hand. I stroked his other between my own.

"I'm a witch, remember?" I wanted him to look up at that comment and see me. I wanted him to see how serious I was and feel reassured by it, but he didn't. He kept his head buried in his hand. "I did it when Master Thomas and I met the other vampires at Theodora's that night, and it worked perfectly, and if that doesn't work, I can do what I did tonight to you, and to Clay a few weeks ago."

"And it works?"

"It did just now, didn't it?"

Nathan didn't answer verbally, but he looked up. The pain of the memory of what had happened still tore at his face. We all sat there in quiet for a while, just letting Nathan process things. Theodora said silence would be the great healer here. The more Nathan processed and adjusted to his new life, the better. He needed to get past the emotional shock of the moment, or moments as it was in this case, and really understand. When he finally leaned back in the chair, I felt he was coming around. He still didn't look like the old Nathan, or even the vampire Nathan who had just woken up yesterday. He was still heavily distressed. I could see it and feel it in how vacant his touch felt when he rubbed my hand as I held his.

"How long does it take? How long does it take to feel normal again?"

Blank stares were in abundance in the parlor. No one had an answer, least of all me. I felt anything but normal, and even then, I was so far away from normal I wasn't sure I could even use that word. It was a fact that I knew Nathan needed to hear, but I also knew I didn't have the heart to tell him. How badly he needed someone to say he would feel normal in just a few days, or weeks, was clear on his face. I felt a true terror about telling him and ruining all Theodora had done to calm him down earlier. I didn't want to be the one, but I had to be. It had to be me. He was my boyfriend, and most importantly, he was like this now because of me. I owed that to him. Even if it set him back, which I didn't doubt it would. That smile I had seen reappear a few times tonight would be gone again. I just had to swallow it deep, do it, and deal with the consequences later.

"Define normal?" asked a voice from heaven. Hearing it lifted the weight of the dread I felt. Nathan looked at Kevin Bolden standing in the door with his wife. Marie and Theodora were behind them. "Seriously Nathan, define normal. What do you believe normal feels like?"

Nathan appeared dumbfounded by Kevin's question, as did the rest of us.

"It's difficult to answer, is it?" asked Kevin. His question appeared directed at more than Nathan. We were once again the students and class was in session. "Ignore what you know about your situation. How do you feel that is different from normal? Mike, in what way do you feel any different from how you did before?"

Mike looked like someone had punched him. His mouth hung open. I hoped that was a sign he was working the problem in his head, but it was Mike. He gave no outward signs of being a deep and introspective person. "I don't know," was his answer, but coming out of his mouth, it sounded like more of a question.

"Apryl, what about you?"

Even Apryl hesitated with her answer. She looked perplexed.

"Oh, come on," urged Kevin. "Anyone? Really think about this."

"I don't feel any different now than I did before," responded Brad.

"Exactly..." Kevin Bolden started to celebrate the response, but Brad quickly interrupted with more to his answer.

"But, at first, I did. I felt like a raw nerve, irritated by the simplest of sensation, and my impulses were stronger, sending me from calm to aggressive in the blink of an eye."

"That's an excellent answer, Brad. See if each of you search your feelings. You'll have what you need to help Nathan and others through these issues. The secret is your own experiences. We are a community. We have to help each other. No one else can." Kevin looked right at Nathan and stepped into the room. "It's just going to take time, Nathan, and then you will feel what you believe is normal again. Look around you. See all the people that have gone through this. Lean on us."

Thank you, Mr. Bolden. Not only did he save me there, but he also opened a door I could walk right through.

"Nathan... lean on me. Let me help you through this." My hand caressed his, and I waited to feel that squeeze of recognition or to see him looking into my eyes, wanting to pull what strength I had to help him. I had to be strong for him. Which meant I needed to hide what a mess I was on the inside from him, and our other little secret. Even if just for a little while, or until I understood it more. Nathan was dealing with so much right now. Telling him he was going to be a father, especially when I couldn't explain how, might be a touch too much. There was still time.

Nathan's head turned toward me. Here it came. He was finally going to look at me. He was finally going to see me as his rock to help him through this. We would tackle this together, just like I wanted to take on any challenges we face for the rest of time. Come on, turn a little more and look at me. See the strength I have in my eyes? Those black, emotionless eyes that are staring up at you beseeching you to let me help you. Yes, he's almost there.

"Lean on all of us Nathan," commented Theodora from the doorway, drawing Nathan's eyes right to her.

If my looks could kill, that woman would be in a casket.

I felt the little squeeze from his hand, and then he finally looked down at me. He looked lost and confused, and why wouldn't he be? He was new in this strange new world.

"It's going to be okay," I said.

"I need to apologize to Amy."

Well, that could be a problem. I doubted Steve and Stan would allow us anywhere near her at the moment, but I couldn't tell Nathan that. He felt bad enough as it was. "Just give her some time. We can talk to her when she wakes up."

"Okay," he agreed reluctantly.

"Why don't you go take a shower? Clean your body and your head." I stood up, pulling his hand with me, and he stood up and followed as I led him out of the room.

Laura grabbed my shoulder before we reached the door.

"Just because you have yours, don't ruin things for me." There was venom in her words, and I caught her glance down at my belly, and it hit me. The realization of what it meant knocked me for a loop. She let go, and I pulled Nathan through the door.

"What was that about?" he asked.

I didn't answer, and pulled him up the stairs and to the bathroom.

Nathan stood there, silently, as I ran his water. A hot shower always helped clear my mind. Not to mention, having him do something normal might help him. It's not like he could sit down and eat a greasy hamburger and fries, or gorge on junk food while watching TV, like he used to do before. Which I never really understood, well maybe I did. There was the bacon. He needed to do as many things he used to do as possible.

Once the water was hot enough, I laid out a towel and started for the door. "Take your time. We won't run out of hot water."

He replied, "Good," and then grabbed my wrist. "I wouldn't want us to get cold." He pulled me in close and kissed me, and boom. Holy Jesus Christ, and what the Hell, all rolled into one. There were fireworks, sparks, and explosions the moment our lips touched. He let go first, and I tried to pull him back in, but not before Nathan said, "He was right."

"What? Who?" I asked weakly. My mouth searched for his. Each attempt to find his missed.

"Mike."

"Mike what?" I asked. My lips finally found his, and there it was again. The fuse was lit, and I was ready to explode, but Nathan pulled back again and held just a hair's width away. His body shuddered. "He said it was more intense," the last word barely making it out before he pulled me in closer, and then pulled me into the shower with him, clothes, and all. It wasn't long before those were nothing more than a wet pile of fabric on the floor, and he hoisted me up in his arms, feeling more alive than I had ever felt in my life.

8

That magic smile returned to Nathan's face. It was my sun, and the world felt warmer with it present. His eyes kept watching me as I dried off, but he wasn't the only one doing some watching. I was watching him. This was only the second time I had seen Nathan naked, make that the second and a half. I had walked in on him once. There was something about him now. Maybe it was the glow left over from what I could only call an electrifying experience. Even without the sun kissed tan he had; he was a feast for the eyes. Best of all, this is how Nathan would look for the rest of his life.

I found myself lost in my own bliss and hoped this would help put him over the hump. Maybe feeling us together, better than ever, would keep him from missing anything or feeling depressed about what he had lost. There was so much more that he had gained, some of which I didn't even know existed. I jumped when his arms wrapped around my waist, and then I allowed myself to sink back into him. If I could have sunk further and become one with him, I would have. There was nothing that sounded better than that union. His hands caressed my skin lightly, and I felt the desire in his fingertips as they roamed. I closed my eyes and let the feeling consume me. They didn't pause as they traced the shape of my body, teasing every inch of me, and I had a feeling he knew exactly what he was doing to me. How he returned to several spots of my body confirmed it, and no matter how much I tried to hold still, my body betrayed me and quivered. Then I froze.

His hands stopped on my stomach and stayed there. They were no longer caressing. Instead, they were just... well.. there. I let my eyes open and looked down. My stomach was no longer flat and taut, like it had been for years. There was a paunch there. If he noticed, this was going to be more than a little problem. I wasn't ready to tell him yet. He needed more time to adjust, and I needed more time to understand how this happened. My only saving grace sat with the fact that he had only seen me naked once before. Maybe, just maybe, he didn't see, or remember, what I looked like then.

Inside, I begged for his hands to move, but they didn't. They just stayed there while he stood behind me. Before he was nuzzling against my neck, but even that had stopped. My gaze drifted up and met the reflection of his in the mirror. I didn't wait long enough to read him. I didn't want to. I didn't want to know if he had noticed and had a question there. My own hands met his and pried them off just enough to allow me to spin around and meet him face to face. Again, our lips met, and that electricity was there. I pushed the kiss deeper, hoping it would chase away anything he may have noticed. I was pretty sure this would work. The heavenly bliss was already making it hard for me to remember why I was doing this. I almost didn't care why anymore as he led me back over to the bed and leaned back.

I laid there in his arms, realizing I could lie here forever and not have a care in the world, and that didn't sound all that bad. What would be wrong about a life lived in bliss? I was sure somewhere someone was living life just that way. Why shouldn't we? The complications of our lives, that's why, answered my mind, and I wanted to yell at it to hush. By now, I had learned enough to realize that if I rolled over and kissed Nathan again, I could chase all of those issues away for another brief period of time. If I kissed him well enough, that period could be extended, but that solved nothing, and I had this nagging feeling of responsibility sneaking its way back in, dragging dread with it by the hair. What I needed to fix or do was too long to list, or at least a list I didn't want to play in my head at the moment.

I rolled over and swung my legs out of the bed and looked up at the clock. A panic reminded me of one of the issues with being what we were. Time wasn't the same for us as it is for others. Not that we had more hours in the day or anything, but being immortal, the feeling of five minutes to us, was not the same as to someone that only lives 80 years or so. The last four hours felt like just minutes, heavenly minutes, but still just minutes, and I had missed an appointment, more of a promise I had made. Nathan's hand reached for my back as I stood up.

"Don't leave," he begged.

"I have to. I promised to meet with Master Thomas this morning," I said and quickly got dressed the traditional way.

"Witch stuff," scoffed Nathan, as he did the same.

"Yes, witch stuff. I am a witch, and part of the problem out there is related to witches. So, yes." I ignored his scoff and finished getting dressed. "I won't be gone long. I will ask Mike and Clay to…" I caught myself before I completed the statement. I realized how it sounded in my head, but I had already sent enough that any reasonable person in Nathan's situation could make the leap.

"In case I get out of control again?"

"Yes," I said, regretting I even brought it up. I could have just asked them to help without Nathan even knowing it. The left over buzz of our bliss dripped away from his face, and seeing it stole mine along with it.

I walked over and placed a hand on his cheek. When he tried to turn away from me, I grabbed the other side of his face to take control of the situation and help center him. "Look, it is just for a bit. I promise, it won't be long before you have control over everything."

He tried to pull away from me, but I maintained my grip, knowing now I couldn't hurt or even bruise him. It was quite the opposite. "Nathan, don't do that. Don't get frustrated, that will just lead to other emotions boiling over. The best thing for you now is to stay calm, and work past this period with the help of all of us. You heard Mr. Bolden." His body relaxed and conveyed his agreement. "I won't be long, and tonight I want to take you some place I used to love going at night around here. Just the two of us, okay?"

"All right."

I gave him a quick kiss, emphasizing on the quickness of it to avoid being pulled back in, and then departed while he pulled his shirt on over his head. I went down the stairs, looking for the first of the two stops I needed to make, on my way out to meet with Master Thomas and Mr. Meridian. I found the second of my stops first, standing out on the porch under the eaves and out of the sun.

"I got to admit Larissa. This is a real nice farm here. Peaceful and beautiful," said Mike as he looked out at the property. "That is, if you ignore the two large camps of opposing forces," he added sarcastically. Both Jeremy and Clay snickered from the rockers they sat in.

"Then let me show you something." I walked up next to Mike and slid my hand over his eyes.

"You going to push me over or something?" he asked. There was a leeriness in his voice that I found humorous. He was actually frightened of me.

"No, just watch." When I removed my hand, I heard a gasp from him. He then walked out of the shadows and out into the sun, taking the tingling sensation that came with it without even a wince. "That is what it looked like when I was a child." Okay, the picture I projected for him may have been a memory from spring and not winter, so sue me, but it looked great.

"I want to see it," demanded Clay as he pounced out of the rocker.

Jeremy followed with a "Me too."

Why not? I thought, and I grabbed Clay by the arm and put him next to Jeremy. Then, from behind, I reached around them with both hands and covered their eyes and performed the same glamor trick on them than I had on Mike. All three were now seeing the same image. Field after field of lavender and lilac in bloom. Tractor rows clearly cut through the field, and every building on the property was newly painted and well maintained, not that I hadn't already fixed those after I arrived.

I let them spend about a minute in that memory before it disappeared, revealing the real world before them.

"Mike's right Larissa. It is a sight to behold," said Jeremy. It was heartfelt, and I slapped him on the back as his head turned in my direction when he said it.

"Thanks. I need to ask a favor of you three."

"Watch Nathan?" asked Mike.

"Yep, can you?"

"We were already planning on it. We discussed it with Mr. Bolden after you two went upstairs. We have him. You don't need to worry about anything."

"Good. Thanks." I said and started for the stairs, but then I stopped and headed back for Mike. I placed a hand on his shoulder and leaned up and whispered into his ear, "And thanks for what you told Nathan."

Mike grinned from ear to ear before he covered his mouth with his hand. I was smiling too as I left the porch, but I wasn't about to turn to let any of them see it.

Out in the old lavender fields, which didn't look anywhere near as well kept and bright as they did in what I had just shown Mike and the others, I spied my next stop.

Seeing Amy running around the fields holding the doll I gave her for Christmas, chasing a dog, make that a wolf, was an adorable and somewhat normal scene. Rob had let his wolfy side out for the moment and bounced around like a hyper puppy. If he rolled over and let her give him a belly rub, I would lose it. I did a quick check and saw both Stan and Steve not far away with Cynthia. They were keeping a watchful eye over things, but neither appeared too concerned with my presence, at least not at the moment.

When Amy saw me, she didn't run to me like she usually did, and that hurt. It told me something had changed between us. She didn't run from me either. I kneeled down and straightened up her clothes with a tug here and a tug there, while Rob stood behind her. I looked him right in the eye. I needed him to know I wasn't there to harm Amy. That it was quite the opposite. He didn't appear all that concerned.

"Is Nathan okay?" Amy asked. Her voice quivered and trailed off.

"Yes," I said, and it wasn't a lie. He was and eventually would be even better. "He is just different now," I added, thinking that explaining the birds and the bees might be easier than this.

"So, he's like you now?"

I nodded. "He is exactly like me and Mike, Clay, Apryl, Jeremy, Brad, Mr. and Mrs. Bolden, and Laura. So, there isn't anything to worry about, or to be frightened of." Well, there was, and I struggled with how to describe it without making her fearful. The truth. They say that never hurts, which they are wrong about that. I have been told the truth many times, and it skewered me. "It's just all new to him, so he needs to understand what all he is feeling and how to deal with it, but," I quickly added. "It won't be long before he is the Nathan you remember, and we can get back to sitting on the porch reading stories and all, okay?"

It was her turn to nod, but what I didn't see was that infectious little girl smile.

"Everything will be all right, honey." I reached up and stroked her hair.

"Will you still have room for me?" she asked, with the question slapping me right across the face.

"Of course. What makes you think I wouldn't?" I asked.

"The baby," she said, and I about fell backwards on my ass. Behind her, Rob phased back into his human form and stepped up close behind her.

"Yes, of course we will darling," I responded.

"Amy, just think of it like having a little brother or sister," Rob pointed out. "It's great. I can't imagine life without my brothers."

"But we aren't real brothers or sisters. I'm not really your child." Her bottom lip quivered, and my heart sank hearing those words.

I pulled her in for a hug and didn't even check to see if Steve or Stan would have a problem with it. If they were over there glaring at me like Ms. Parrish used to, I didn't care. "Amy, stop thinking like that. You are our child in every way that matters, and that is all that is important."

"And I'm your uncle," added Rob.

"Yep, and Rob is your uncle," I agreed. "Every family has one of those crazy uncles."

Amy giggled, and that was what I needed to hear. I kissed her on the forehead and stood up. "Now you play with Rob, and I will be back later. I need to go meet with some witches." She hugged my leg.

"Mike and the others will watch him today."

"Jack can't do your little trick to make him think he is somewhere else?" asked Rob.

I shook my head. "Not yet. It takes practice, which is where I am heading. More witch training."

"More school? Didn't we just leave a school?"

I just shrugged as I turned and walked away. I didn't make it more than a few steps before I heard the squeals of happiness behind me.

9

Marcus Meridian's little watch dogs out front didn't even raise an amber flecked eye when I passed them and approached the tent's opening. I paused with my hand on the canvas of the tent and looked at each of them for some kind of reaction. They sat of to the side on old wooden crates playing cards and acted like they didn't even notice me, but I saw the side glances they gave me. One finally looked up from his cards and with a deep chested chuckle said, "Go on in, you're late."

I pulled the canvas flap open and stepped into his chalet, just like before. I had to wonder if all the other tents were the same. Did they lead to some other place?

"Master Thomas, I'm sorry I'm late. Time got away from me." He sat alone on the sofa, waiting.

"It's fine Larissa," responded Marcus Meridian from the hall to my left. "Oh, and he isn't a Master anymore, and you are not a witch. At least not one the council recognizes." He waved a folded piece of paper with a wax seal out in the air in front of him. "When did this arrive?" he asked Master Thomas.

"This morning."

"Shall I?" prompted Marcus.

Master Thomas didn't respond. He just sat there, almost looking annoyed.

Marcus unfolded the paper and held it out in front of him at arm's length. He gave the paper a little pop and then cleared his throat with an over-exaggerated cough.

"It is the decision of the council that Master Benjamin Thomas be stripped of his seat on the council and all the rights and duties adorned to him. He is now exiled from our community."

The world fell in on me. This was another life that I had a hand in destroying. I turned and apologized, "I'm sorry–" but Marcus interrupted me.

"Oh, just wait."

"Larissa, I knew what I was getting involved in. I did this knowing full well what could happen, and I was prepared. This changes nothing, it's just hot air."

"Can I continue?" asked Marcus. He popped the paper with a finger.

Master Thomas and I both turned our attention back to Marcus. "It is also the council's decision that Larissa Dubois be exiled and categorized as a hostile element in the magic community. She is to be apprehended and transported to Mordin as soon as possible." He closed the paper and balled it up. "Oh, it's signed, Supreme

Wintercrest." He tossed the ball of paper up into the air, and it burst into flames, burning up before it hit the ground behind him. "So, now shall we get started?"

I fell down to my knees, surprised the ground was there to catch me. The world felt like someone had yanked it out from under me.

"Oh, come now Larissa," commented Marcus. "Welcome to the club." He extended his hand and helped me back up to my feet. "Everyone here is an exile. That is why we are here, and there are many more of us out in the world. Anyone that doesn't kiss the ass of Madame Wintercrest, or the council, are considered such. This changes nothing. It actually makes things better."

"Um, how so?" I asked, more than a little curious how my being called a hostile magic entity and to be sent some place called Mordin made things better. I didn't even know what that was. "And what the hell is Mordin?"

"Oh good. Get mad," Marcus said as he sat down next to Master Thomas. "I knew I liked this one." He smiled like a proud parent.

"Mordin is the prison for witches and other magicals. Like the Coven, it exists between the real world and the magical world. Those that have committed crimes against—"

"Those that are the biggest threat," interjected Marcus.

"... crimes against the rules of our community, or against another witch are there," completed Master Thomas.

My body shook under me, and I felt I was about to hit the floor again and moved over to a chair and used the back for support as my mind kept repeating that word repeatedly. Prison! Make that a magic prison! What is that?

"It's nothing to worry about," Marcus dismissed flippantly.

"It's everything to worry about," disagreed Master Thomas.

"Nah," retorted Marcus.

"If she is there, she can't do anything she needs to do."

"True," said Marcus as he rolled up off the sofa and stormed toward the door. "Come on," he said and yanked my arm when he passed by. "You too, Ben."

We walked outside and his guard dogs immediately snapped to attention and everyone in eyesight went down on a bended knee. Marcus let out a loud sigh at the sight. "Up! Get up!" His voice echoed across the land. Everyone stood. "Let's hear it. What do you think of Mordin?"

There was a loud grumble across the camp.

"Okay, that's unanimous. No one likes it." He turned and remarked to Master Thomas and me, "but watch this."

"Who here has been sentenced by the council to be sent to Mordin?" He raised his hand and turned his back on the crowd and faced me. Every single person in camp behind him raised one of their hands. Marcus walked back into his tent with his hand still up in the air.

I stood there and took in the scene until the crowd dispersed. There were dozens, if not hundreds, of people here. All sentenced by the council and considered criminals of some kind. I had to wonder what their crimes were, but that was probably a question I couldn't walk right up to someone and ask. That didn't stop me from wondering as I made eye contact with a few of them before I went back inside.

"Any more questions?" Marcus asked. He sat casually on the sofa waiting on our return.

I had a ton of them, but none I felt comfortable asking.

"That doesn't dismiss the threat of Mordin," stated Master Thomas. "It is a very real place, and it houses some of the worst criminals of our world." He looked at Marcus Meridian sternly. "And I'm not talking about those that have crossed the council, I am talking about those that use magic to murder and terrorize. Neither is to be tolerated in our world."

"No disagreement there, Ben. I just wanted to show that the threat of imprisonment is one of Mrs. Wintercrest's favorite tools, and she uses it against anyone that might push back or become a pebble in her shoe. I think Larissa has made it more than a little uncomfortable for her and I find that absolutely fascinating." Marcus examined me with a curious gaze. "Shall we find out what she can do?"

He again got up and walked past me and toward the door, where he waited.

"Well, that is what you are here for, isn't it?" Marcus asked.

To be honest, I wasn't sure why I was here anymore. Let me see if I can sum up my current status. I was being hunted by an old vampire, who was still alive. I came here to confront him, and did, only to be stopped from killing him by the Council of Mage's Supreme. My boyfriend was attacked and is now a vampire. I am now an exile and criminal with a prison cell waiting for me. These two, basically magic royalty and Master Thomas, want me to save the world, and I am also pregnant, which who-the-hell knows how that is even possible. That about summed it up.

Marcus walked through the camp, and everyone he passed kneeled or bowed. He asked them to stop a few times, but eventually gave up with a headshake and continued out beyond the edge of camp and into a field.

Something familiar caught my eye around a campfire off in the distance. There, with a group of six other rogue witches, laughing and smiling, were Jack and Lisa. It felt good to see them with what I guess we could call our cousins, much like how Theodora had referred to the other vampires. They needed to be around others like them, their own tribe. This would help them grow. God knows I was letting them down in that responsibility. I was too consumed in my world to help them grow as witches.

"Stand here," instructed Marcus. This reminded me of a session with Mr. Helms or Master Nevers, so I readied myself for anything.

He kept walking and Master Thomas stayed with him. They were talking between themselves. Marcus was asking how much I knew, and Master Thomas was trying to explain what he had covered so far, but then he said I was still raw, and that hit a big inflamed raw nerve within me.

"You know I can hear you."

"Yes, we do," Marcus echoed back.

The two men stopped and kept their back to me as they talked. Their discussion was now a whisper or something lower. I couldn't hear them, which at this distance I should be able to hear them clearly, but there was something else missing. I couldn't hear or feel their heartbeats. Tricky, tricky witches. I adjusted my stance.

Marcus spun around and slung a fireball in my direction, but I was ready for it, and I didn't just deflect it like any witch would. That would be too simple and elementary. I wanted to impress him. To truly show him what I could do. I felt the vibrations around me and squeezed them together, trapping the fire ball halfway between us. It hung there in the air, spinning and pulsating. I looked over it at the two men and felt pretty proud of myself. He probably expected me to just move out of the way, or deflect it with one of my own. Not pull out what I felt was some advanced stuff they don't teach anymore. I did everything but bow before Marcus flipped his wrist and I got knocked over by a flash.

"Don't assume your opponent doesn't understand the fabric of the world, too. Everything you can do, can be undone."

I picked myself up off the ground and brushed the grass off of my jeans while I listened and fully understood what I assumed was lesson number one. Out of the corner of my eye, I picked up some movement around the front of the house. It was Nathan, Mike and Clay leaving and heading out into the vampire camp. That wasn't exactly what I had in mind when I asked them to watch him, but maybe this was a good thing. Nathan's visit out there yesterday seemed to help him cope. They hit the tree line, and a few vampires came out to meet them. The greetings were friendly, but one was a little too friendly for my comfort. The hug Theodora gave Nathan appeared to last a little longer than acquaintance level. It was more in the realm of close personal friend, or more. I watched as her hand lingered on his shoulder as she introduced him around. I was so focused on them; I didn't notice the long line of others leaving the house for the woods, led by Kevin and Jen Bolden, followed by Marie Norton with Pam and Jeremy bringing up the rear. Theodora didn't greet any of them with the same warmth she had Nathan. I felt something burning inside me, and even my skin felt warm, and it was getting hotter. A fireball knocked me to the ground, and I rolled around, putting out a few flames on my clothes and in my hair.

"She's good, but raw," I heard Master Thomas remark.

"I see," chuckled Marcus. "Get up. Get up," he commanded and waited while I stood up, calculating how and when I would get him back for that.

"Now try to hurt me," commanded Marcus. He stood facing me, with his arms crossed in front of him.

"What?" I asked, not exactly understanding what he wanted me to do.

"You heard me."

"All right," I agreed, rather reluctantly. I wasn't sure he really knew what he was asking. He might not be able to defend himself because I was faster than most witches. I added a little flare and spun around, slinging my own in his direction. The man never even moved, and my attack veered off into the ground beside him.

"Not attack me. Try to hurt me. Do you understand?"

I didn't, but a feeling I hadn't felt in years soon remedied that. A paralyzing sensation sent me to the ground. My insides were being squeezed. The uncomfortable pressure graduated to full on pain, which was a sensation I hadn't missed. My hands clawed at my body to find the source, but there was nothing. Then, as quick as it came on, it all stopped.

"Do you understand now?" Marcus asked.

I pushed up on my elbows but still struggled to speak. The memory of the pain I had just felt was still fresh and caused me to groan with each movement I made to get back to my feet.

"We haven't covered that yet," Master Thomas said.

"What exactly are they teaching in covens these days?" sniped Marcus Meridian. He seemed to enjoy this. "How about some of elemental magic? Let's try this."

The ground rumbled underneath me and started to glow. A crack opened up. I jumped to avoid being swallowed, but weeds and blades of grass grew up and grabbed me, pulling me back toward the crevasse that had formed. My fingers clawed at the ground, but I slipped closer to the edge. I had had it with the games, and my mind drew a combined symbol made up for the solar cross and besom. One of the few combinations I had already figured out, thanks to my father's notes. The hole closed, and the weeds turned brown. In the distance, Marcus Meridian hit the ground, and Master Thomas laughed smugly.

"You can thank her father for that."

"Yea well. I won't let that happen again," Marcus brushed off his black slacks, and then rolled up the sleeves of his white shirt. "Not bad Larissa. Not bad at all. You can make your own magic. I'm impressed."

"Thank you," I said, then the ground rolled toward me, but stopped just short of me, and again Marcus fell to the ground.

"I should have told you; her runes are strong." Now it was Master Thomas who seemed to enjoy this more than anyone. He reached down and helped up his counterpart. "Larissa, go ahead and drop it."

I did as he requested and let the symbols leave my thought.

"Okay. That's good to know." Marcus shot a look at Master Thomas and then walked away from him, putting distance between him. "That's actually very good Larissa. It means your ability to apply curses and enchant objects is very strong. How about your potions? Have you mastered that?" He continued to walk, now circling around me, almost stalking.

"I know some basics, but I have not mastered it. That I am sure of."

"Good, knowing your limits is very important. I have people that can help you with that. What about spells?"

My mind went back to Mrs. Saxon's on Elemental Spells 1 and 2, and the ones my mother taught me. I felt I had a good handle on them, but in this company, I had to wonder. "I know a few."

"Like what? Humor me."

I was better at doing them than listing them. Kind of like a spelling test in normal school classes. I knew when a word was spelled correctly, but don't ask me to be the one to spell it. I had to think. A few came right to mind. "Teleportation. Levitation. Glamor."

"Good, those are important ones, and there are many variations of each of those. Tell me, do you still say the words that go with it?"

I shook my head.

"Thank god," he said and threw his hands up exasperated. "Too many young witches pay attention to the movies. It's a wonder they aren't all running around with sticks waving them when they cast a spell nowadays." His hand made wild circles in the air, but then stopped and pointed right at me. "But you, you aren't a young witch, and you have great promise. But what do you say? Let's stop messing around."

This was messing around? I was confused. He was acting like the test hadn't even begun. Was this just fun for him?

"Take that rock there, on the ground beside you, and throw it at me." Marcus wagged a finger and then cautioned me, "Don't use your hands."

I looked down at the rock. It was rather small, but size had nothing to do with his request. At least I didn't believe so.

"Come on. Don't look at it. Pick it up and throw it," he urged. Master Thomas watched curiously, and I looked at him for support. If I really threw it at Marcus, I wasn't sure he could get out of the way in time. "Do it!" Marcus ordered.

The rock lifted off the ground and then propelled itself toward Marcus Meridian. It never got close to him before he dismissed it with a simple wave of the hand, but that didn't mean he didn't jump out of the way.

"One," said Master Thomas. He held up a single finger on his hand.

"Yep, but that was a simple one. If she couldn't do that, she couldn't really call herself a witch, could she?"

Master Thomas smirked.

"And, actually, that is two," Marcus corrected Master Thomas. "Pyrokinesis."

"True," he agreed, and raised another finger.

"Two?" I turned to Master Thomas and asked.

He held the fingers out in my direction as if I needed to see them clearer. I knew the count was two, but two what, and why were they counting?

"Pay attention." He said and pointed toward Marcus Meridian.

If I wasn't annoyed before, I was more than a little annoyed when that rock flew back at my head. I moved and felt foolish when it stopped and fell several feet short of me. I shot two quick looks at both Marcus and Master Thomas. Each was unapologetic, and that just turned my heat up a little more.

"Turn that rock into a tree," ordered Marcus.

At that moment, I would rather melt it down and send half of it at each of them. I stood over the rock, looking down at it, and then at the two of them. Then back at the rock.

"Larissa, do you know how to change one thing to another?"

"Yes," I barked back. I did. My mother had taught me, and that was why I always had roses for my mother on Mother's Day, even though we grew nothing but lavender and lilac on the farm.

"Well, then, we are waiting."

I looked down at the ugly rock. It was gray and lifeless. Just like the stone floor in Mr. Demius' classroom. The same floor that I turned into a thick, lush carpet of green grass. I leaned down over it, and closed my eyes, and imagined the elemental symbol of fire, just like I always had before. A flash emitted from my hand toward the rock, and the ground around it changed. Roots extended out and into the ground. Then the trunk projected up, and the first branch took shape, forking off at the top. It continued to grow until it was taller than me, and the first leaves sprouted, giving it the look of a tree in early spring, not the dead of winter like the ones that surrounded my farm.

A third finger on Master Thomas' hand went up. "I think we can pass on number four. I've heard from others she has done it before."

"Nope, I need to see it."

"Oh geez," sighed Master Thomas. His shoulders slumped.

"I won't let her do too much."

Both hands extended out palm up and then dropped to his side. "Do your worst," he said, sounding resigned to his fate, but why did I feel his fate was now in my hands?

"Larissa, I want you to make Ben dance. Not by moving his arms and legs, but by controlling his mind."

"You mean consumption?"

"Now that's a term I haven't heard in years, but yep, that is what I mean. Make our pal Ben there do the Charleston or some modern dance kids do today."

I looked at Master Thomas apologetically. I didn't enjoy doing this. The only times I had done this before were for schoolwork, but technically, this was. It was a test, but that didn't mean I enjoyed the thought of doing this to someone I looked up to. It didn't take much to plant the thought in his head. No Charleston, or modern dance. Just a little soft shoe style shuffling of his feet, with a new arrangement of fingers on his hand. It no longer showed three fingers, but now a single one, the middle, was pointed up in the air. I didn't keep control of Master Thomas long, just enough to make my point.

When I released him, Marcus Meridian conceded, "that's four."

"Four what?" I asked.

"Four of the seven wonders," replied Marcus.

"What?" Wonders? What the hell was he talking about? We were witches, not God. I knew what the seven wonders were. In fact, there were two sets. The ancient and modern ones, and none of them had anything to do with what I just did. The only wonder I felt about any of this was about why I was being asked to perform them.

"The test of the Seven Wonders. Larissa, if you are going to challenge for Supreme, you better know the test of the seven wonders. You have just finished four of them: telekinesis, transmutation, pyrokinesis, and concilium, or what you called consumption. There are three left, which I don't doubt you can perform. That is with the right training. They are a little more advanced and need to be performed in more supervised settings than this."

"What are those wonders?" I asked.

"Divination, Descensum, and Vitalum Vitalis," Marcus spouted.

"Diva-whats-it, Dec-a-whose it, and... can I have that in English?"

"Divination is the ability to see or have knowledge of the future," Master Thomas stepped forward and began his explanation in an academic tone. It reminded me of the many times he and Mr. Demius conducted my secret classes. "Descensum is astral projection to send your soul to the nether plane. Lisa might be able to help you with that."

"Good, I never once cracked the stack of books Edward placed next to my bed on the topic." I neglected to bring up the warning he gave me about how dangerous it was to try.

"Now she has performed the last one. I was there."

This seemed to surprise Marcus. His stalking of me, his prey, stopped, and he turned to Master Thomas and pressed a single finger to his lips. It remained there until he spoke. "Are you serious?"

"What is the last one? The Vital Vitamins thing?" My attempt to pronounce whatever the double-V item was, appeared to humor both Marcus and Master Thomas.

"Vitalum Vitalis," repeated Marcus Meridian. "It's the hardest of all the wonders. It's the ability to create life."

"The duck," I mumbled.

"Yep, the duck," repeated Master Thomas. He then continued to explain the incident to Marcus Meridian, who seemed to be in a state of disbelief and asked Master Thomas to repeat and explain several parts. Inside, I was no longer thinking of the duck. I was considering another possibility.

10

After a few more rounds of the game Marcus-says, we returned to the camp so Marcus could, as he said, make several formal introductions. That didn't mean I wasn't also subjected to dozens of other less formal ones as we walked through the camp. Everywhere we walked, people greeted and gushed over Marcus and Master. The welcomes I received bordered on downright frigid. No where even close to the warm welcoming I saw Nathan receive out in the tree line moments earlier.

Things didn't change much once we reached the first person Marcus said I needed to meet. She was a peculiar-looking lady. Her brown hair sat atop her head in tight curls, clearing her glum face of any hair, giving me a clear view of her bright green cutting eyes and her rather small mouth. It just hung there on her face, pinched together. Her leather boots and long-sleeved reddish brown gown looked out of place in modern fashion. Like me, she appeared to be a woman time had forgotten, though her attire would have fit more in a time well before my own. She wore white gloves on her hands with the fingers removed. Her name was Mary Smith.

I reached my hand forward when Marcus made the introduction, and in return, I received a once over, and not a pleasant one at that. There was a scoff that accompanied it.

"Mary Smith will help you with astral projection." Her death-like glare appeared to disagree with Marcus's offer, though she didn't protest, and by the way she bowed at his request, which Marcus sighed at, she would run into a raging fire if he asked her to.

"James," bellowed Marcus.

A man with long dark hair three tents down stood up. He stepped out away from the group he had been sitting with and sprinted towards us with dozens of eyes following him. On closer inspection, I was a little surprised. This man wasn't much more than a boy. He couldn't be much older than I was, or was supposed to be. With a rare chance, he could be early twenties and just look young. He was slim, making his skinny jeans a tad bit baggy on him. He wore a bright red hoodie over a white tee and sneakers. There was nothing witchy looking about him.

"Still working the streets?" Marcus asked as the two men exchanged handshakes.

"Some, but I keep it fair." He flashed a killer smile at Marcus.

"Larissa, meet James O'Conner, street swindler."

"Hey now, I take offense to that word." James laughed and extended a hand to me. His welcoming was a tad warmer than old Mary back there. She was still glaring in my direction. "You can call me a hustler or vendor, but never a swindler."

"My mistake. James here will be your guide to divination."

There he was with the big words again, and I had forgotten to take notes, which explained the blank expression on my face.

"The ability to see the future," Marcus leaned forward to explain. "James here runs local shell and card games on the street."

"But," James interrupted and stepped in front of Marcus. He slapped his hands together and displayed that killer smile again. "I never, and I do mean never, use any magic during my little profession, but if you need to learn how to see things that hadn't happened yet, I'm at your service." He spread his arms out wide and curtsied, and remained bent over.

"I guess I do," I admitted, reluctantly.

"You absolutely do." Marcus grabbed me by the arm and rushed me away. I looked back behind us, and James was still bent over. "And you need to perfect your potions."

We walked deeper into the camp and up to a tattered tent. Marcus didn't stop at the door, and pulled me through the opening. Where we emerged was a room that looked oddly familiar. Shelves cluttered with containers of all varying sizes and colors lined every wall, just like Mrs. Tenderschott's classroom. Then the oddness of the moment went up another notch, when a woman that could have been her twin emerged, and I almost screamed her name.

She gasped and placed a hand over her heart. "Marcus! It's not nice to sneak up on an old woman."

"I know. I'm sorry, Gladys. I have someone I wanted you to meet."

"I see that. You must be Larissa Dubois. You're something of a celebrity around here." She didn't hesitate to walk right up to me and give me a big hug. Once the shock wore off, I did the same. "It's so nice to meet you." She pulled me in closer, not the normal reaction when someone was in the presence of a vampire. Hugs didn't happen often, and definitely not ones this close. When she let go, she kept one arm wrapped around me, and spun to my side so we were both looking at Marcus. "So, I take it this old fart is here because you need help with potions? That is usually the only time he stops by."

"Not true," protested Marcus.

The rotund woman narrowed her eyes and tilted her salt-and-pepper covered head down. It was a universal look that all parents used. I know I had felt it more than once in my life, by both sets of parents.

"Not entirely true," he conceded sheepishly. "I do promise to stop by more often."

"Nonsense, you're a busy man. I just enjoy busting your chin a bit." She leaned over and said in my ear. "Did you enjoy watching him turn red as much as I did?"

"I didn't turn red."

"You did. Didn't he, Larissa?"

"Yep," I agreed because he did, and small beads of sweat formed on his brow. His heart even skipped a few beats.

"Well, any who, I'd be more than happy to help you with potions. Have you had any training?"

"Some," I said.

"Well, some is better than none. We can cover some basics starting tomorrow and get an idea of where you are. Then we go from there. How does that sound?"

"Sounds great," I responded. What else was I going to say? Marcus Meridian, someone who was practically royalty in our world, if you ignored his family's current standing with the council, was assigning people to help tutor me. And none of them were asking why. They were just agreeing to do it, some less enthusiastic than others, but they still agreed.

We stayed and chatted with Gladys for a few minutes. Some of it was what I would call shop talk, which appeared to be an attempt to feel out where I was with potions without actually testing me. Hearing that I understood the purpose of some of the foundational elements seemed to make her happy. It probably meant I had a solid base to start with.

By the time we left her tent, night had fallen, and the moon was high above us. Most of the witches had turned in. The need for sleep did not restrict me like my fellow witches, but that didn't mean I didn't relish the break. There had been something on my mind since Marcus and Master Thomas brought up the seven wonders. In fact, it was around one particular wonder they defined that brought on a full on feeling of panic that I worked to hide from both of them.

"Do you know where Nathan and the others went?" I asked Jack and Rob, sitting in the parlor watching television.

"No, but I heard Apryl saying something about a vampire pirate," responded Lisa as she walked down the hall from the kitchen with an apple in hand. The bruises of her first encounter with Jean St. Claire were still visible. I brushed the hair out of her face to expose more of them. "I'm fine. My ribs barely hurt anymore." She twisted around and then did a quick spin, trying to hold back a wince. But I clearly saw it. "So, what was this about a vampire pirate?" She asked, and took a bite of her apple. Her question had Jack and Rob sitting on the edge of their seats, literally.

"It's a long story, but yes, there is a vampire that used to be a pirate. I'll explain more later. Did they say when they would be back?" I didn't really care when the others would be back, but I wanted to know about Nathan. I had something planned, but also had something I needed to do to clear my mind.

"Nope. They didn't even say bye."

"Hmm." My hands found my hip as I hoped Nathan hadn't forgotten, but that gave me a few moments. "Where is Amy?"

"You'll love this," Rob started as he sat back in the chair and returned his focus to whatever he and Jack were watching on television. "Steve picked up right where Ms. Parrish left off." As if I hadn't noticed. "They're out somewhere refining their skills."

"So be careful about kicking a rock down the road. It might be one of them," remarked Rob with a laugh.

I let his joke go without a comment. I was too focused on what I needed to do next. I turned to Lisa just before she took another bite of her apple. "Is there anyone in the kitchen?"

"Nope, it's all clear. You going to do your visit home thing?"

I nodded.

"One day, I want you to take me with you. I would like to meet the woman who gave birth to you. Family roots are important."

"One day. I promise."

11

"Mom."

"Well, hello there. I was wondering when you might come for a visit." My mother turned around. She was again at the sink, right where she had been every time I visited. That brought a horrifying thought regarding her eternity.

"Mom, you're always at the sink doing the dishes or something when I arrive. Is that where you spend all your time when I'm not here?"

She walked over and took her usual seat at the kitchen table. She had a humorous smirk on her face as she waited for me to do the same. When I finally sat, she gave me her answer. "I don't know. You will have to ask yourself about that. I am where you expect me to be. Is that how you remember me?"

That left me stammering. I searched my mind for any memories of my mother not at the sink. There were plenty. Even more than those when she was at the sink, but then I realized something. There was a unique characteristic about the memories that involved me sitting at the table and my mother at the sink. All were the same, and it was at that moment it all made sense, and it was my turn to have a humorous smirk on my face. "No. I have tons of memories of you doing all sorts of things, but every time I came to you for your advice on magic, life, and even boys, it was here, in this kitchen. I would sit right here, and you would stand at the sink until you would come join me at the table to talk."

She looked down at the table, and then back up at me. "Then that would be why you find me here. It's driven by the reason for your visit. This is all up to you."

"Huh," I replied as I pondered this. "So, if I came here to work in the field, I would find you out there?" I had to ask to be sure I understood how this thing worked.

"Perhaps," said my mother. She leaned across the table and whispered. "But let's not do that. Maybe something where we are sitting on the porch with a cool breeze."

"Deal."

She smiled back, "So since we are here, what are you looking for my advice on today? Is it magic, life, or... boys?"

"Kind of magic and boys," I squirmed. This was not going to be an easy conversation to have.

"Okay, I can help with those. I am kind of an expert in at least one of them. What are your questions or problems?

"Well," I started, beating around the bush, and hemming and hawing. The question sounded simple in my mind, but every time I started to ask it, it took a detour somewhere between that easy spot and my mouth.

"Larissa, what is it? I haven't seen you this uncomfortable since you told me you broke the window in your room."

To a seven-year-old, having to tell on yourself was about as traumatic as it could get, and to be honest, it wasn't my fault. There was a bug on the outside, and I wanted it to move, so I threw my shoe at the window. The bug moved. Oh, for the simpler times.

"Mom, I'm pregnant," I spat out like ripping off a band-aid.

My mom sat straight up, while in slow motion her eyes increased in size, larger than I thought was humanly possible. Her hands went up to her mouth and tried to hide the wide grin that was forming. "My baby is having a baby!" she crowed, and then jumped out of her seat and wrapped her arms around my neck, hugging me. She was surprisingly quick. She kissed my cheek. "This is great news. Congratulations. You and Nathan must be so happy." Then she let go of my neck and backed away and asked, "It is Nathan's, right?"

"Yes, mother!" I exclaimed, shocked she would ask such a question. "What kind of girl do you think I am?"

"Not saying that, and I don't know how long it's been since you last visited. I'm so happy for both of you. I'm sure you are both over the moon about this. I remember how your father reacted when I told him about you…"

"He doesn't know," I said, interrupting her gushing.

"What?" The happiness and glow drained from her, and she sat back in her chair.

"Mom, it's a long story, and a lot has happened."

"Wait, I remember now. What ended up happening with Jean and your plan?"

"It went to hell in a handbasket." And even that was putting a positive spin on it. I sat back in the chair, and my shoulders slumped. Something that happened here without really having to think about it. "There is so much to tell you that you need to know." I let out a loud sigh and collapsed forward onto the table, letting my arms catch my head. The abridged version. "The plan worked, and we removed the curse from New Orleans. Jean walked right into our trap and gave me the conflict I wanted without breaking any witch or vampire rules." Or so I thought. Technically, I still hadn't. It was all self-defense no matter how you looked at it, but with all I know now, why would I expect Mrs. Wintercrest and the council to respect the rules? "Jean got away with the help of Mrs. Wintercrest. Let's leave it at the council and I aren't on the best of terms right now, and all of Jean's followers are camped on one side of the yard out front, and all the rogue witches are on the other." I paused and thought about it for a moment. There was a lot to cover, without going blow by blow into the details of what happened. "Yep, that covers it."

"Oh, dear!" gasped my mother before she covered her mouth with her hands.

"I wouldn't worry too much about any of that. There are some very smart witches helping me, and about as bad as that sounds, that isn't my biggest concern. The pregnancy is."

"Okay. Okay." My mother repeated it a few more times before she calmed down. "I understand. I can help you with that." She took in a deep breath, "What's a mother for?" Her voice shook.

"Mom, I'm not sure you can, but I hope I'm wrong and you can."

"Try me." She straightened herself up and sat with her hands clasped together on the table.

"How is it even possible?"

I saw the same shocked look on her face I had seen on the face of others when I asked that same question. "Larissa, we had that talk. Don't you remember?"

"No mom, it's not that." I wished it were that simple and bowed my head before I explained further. "Mom, think about what I am now. That is the problem. How could this physically happen?"

"Oh," she said, and then she stood up and exclaimed, "Oh!" Her chair skittered across the floor. "How is that possible?"

"I know, right? My body can't change any more. It won't age. It won't get sick. And it most definitely won't change to support a womb and a child."

My mother grabbed her chair and slid it back to the table before sitting back down. "I've heard of the opposite situation, where a male vampire and a human female had a child."

"Dhampir," I interjected.

"Yes, but never this way. I assume you have asked some vampires about this." Question marks dripped from her voice.

"Yep, some that are very old, and they are just as stumped as you are, which is why I came to you."

She looked at me curiously.

"I am not just any woman or vampire, I am also a witch, and do you remember the situation with the baby duck when I was nine?"

"Yes." The single syllable word took several seconds to leave her lips as she glared across the table at me. "Oh Larissa, you didn't? Did you?"

"I don't know... I might have... I don't really remember... but it's possible." I stuttered, trying to remember if I had. "We were–" My lips clamped closed as soon as I realized what I was about to say, and who I was about to say it in front of.

"You were what?"

Why did she have to ask? "We were," I tried, but I still couldn't say it, at least not by name. "We were," I squirmed, trying to complete the phrase, "doing something of a personal nature, and I might have thought about having a baby and family with him at that moment." God, I hoped she understood my cryptic explanation. It was embarrassing enough to say it one time. If I had to repeat it or provide any clarifications, I would just die, if that were possible.

"It takes more than just thinking about it, but," she held up a finger. She had a point to make, and I was all ears. I leaned forward for her expert guidance. "It is possible when you are in the correct mental or emotional state, either distress or elation, for something to slip, but you would have noticed it. Did you feel that flash of warmth as the fire of creation ignited?"

Oh, I felt a flash of warmth all right. I wasn't sure if that was it or not. "I might have." That was as much as I was going to admit to. If that was it, there was something that didn't make any sense. "When it happened before, the duck just appeared in my hands. If that was it, wouldn't a baby just appear there, like the duck?"

"Should have, or I should say, could have. It all depends on what you were thinking about. Maybe you wanted to go through the childbearing process," she suggested. "It's hard to be specific without knowing what you were thinking about at the time."

"That has to be how," I conceded. My thoughts were all over the place, like they usually were. There was no telling what I was thinking and if that idea had slipped into my mind. It was the only explanation, no matter how crazy it might have sounded. I had to accept it. What choice did I really have? I was pregnant. This was really happening, and now I had an explanation of how. The next question in my mind... what the hell was this pregnancy going to be like? Theodora and Marie had already told me vampire pregnancies were accelerated, and in just a day I was already showing. That should have taken weeks. I was probably a few days from not being able to fit through the door. Now the next part of what seemed like a dark daytime soap opera drama, I had to tell Nathan. "That is why I haven't told Nathan yet?"

"You wanted to understand how."

"Not wanted to," I corrected with a shake of my head. "I needed to. He was going to ask. What could I tell him?"

"Do you think he will believe you?" She looked at me cockeyed.

"I think so. He grew up around witches." In reality, I hoped he would. I was still having a hard time believing it myself, but I found myself in an Occam's Razor moment. This was heavily improbable, but all other possibilities had been removed.

"The only other question left is how are you going to tell him? I fixed your father a nice dinner and told him after. You could do the same. It would have a sense of symmetry from generation to generation. Almost a tradition."

Oh, yeah, that was one detail I hadn't shared with my mother yet. That would make that a terrible idea. I shook my head and braced for her reaction. She had to know, and there really wasn't any point in holding it back. "Jean bit Nathan, and Nathan is now a vampire." I paused and let that sink in for a moment, and braced for a load of questions, but the lengthy silence meant there were none. The shock of the news must have knocked them out of her. "He is fine and acclimating to things rather nicely." My mother's face was stone still. No twitching and no blinking. "And, it at least solved a problem. There won't be any awkward eighty-year-old grandfatherly looking man kissing on a teenage girl moments when he aged, and I didn't."

The stone expression on my mother's face cracked slightly, but not entirely. "Well, that's something."

"I already have an idea of how to tell him." Now I just needed Nathan to cooperate.

12

It took quite a while for my mother's shock to wear off, and our conversation return to something of a normal mother daughter chat. Well, scratch that. There was nothing normal about us or our chats, not when you compared them to those others probably had, but we weren't exactly normal. She showed a lot of concern for Nathan and how he was adjusting. I told her about the Boldens and how they were experts in this, and that Theodora had taken a lead. Both pieces of news appeared to make her feel better. Of course, I mentioned many times that he had me to help him. I had over eighty years of experience in being a vampire. This was a point she continually brushed past without so much as a smile or comment.

After I left my mother, with many promises to stop by throughout my pregnancy, I went out in search of Nathan to put my plan for telling him into action, but he was nowhere to be found. My home was quiet, with people sleeping in every room upstairs. Downstairs, the kitchen was dark, which was how I found it when I left my mother. Someone must have turned off the light while I was sitting there. I didn't know why, but Jack, Martin, or Rob seemed to be the most likely suspects to me.

The parlor was the only downstairs room not empty. It was dark, with only the flicker of the television illuminating its sole occupant. I went in and plopped down next to Laura on the sofa. She had the show down low, and the sounds of crickets and the low rumble of the river rode a cool breeze in through the windows.

"Whatcha watching?"

"No clue, whatever that was on when I turned it on. It's not half bad though," she replied without breaking her stare.

I would have never picked Laura for a fantasy romance fan. This had kings, castles, and fancy dresses, and lots of big words that no one would ever say if they weren't trying to mock Shakespeare. And even though I felt like mocking it when I first started watching it–I doth think the girl protest too much–I got lost in it after a few cheesy lines.

"Where are the others?" I asked, staring at the screen, and feeling a little lovelorn for the old days.

"Don't know. Probably out there with Theodora and Marteggo."

"So, you met him?" We were two girls gabbing while watching a sappy romance movie. The only thing missing was a big bowl of popcorn.

"Oh yeah, we all did."

"What did you think?"

I turned and looked at her to see her expression. The flicking light of the television highlighted her naturally beautiful features. She stayed focused on the screen, where the woman, Frances, or some frilly name like that, cried because of the contents of a note a royal messenger handed her. The contents of which were still a mystery to us, adding to the intrigue. "Interesting fellow. Exactly what I would imagine a pirate would be. Tons of ego. Tons of macho attitude, but just enough of a soft edge to swoon someone like Theodora."

She nailed it. That was exactly my read as well.

"He and Mike hit it off instantly and started some stupid macho feats of strength competition or some crap like that. That was when I headed in. Nathan and Clay had joined in when I left."

Somehow, none of that surprised me. Not even hearing that Nathan was involved. He was a guy, and I couldn't remember how many stories he told me of the stupid sports or challenges he, Rob, and Martin engaged in. It was just how guys were wired. They were also wired to win. Jen and I talked about it once, when I complained how stupid it was, and she told me all men, no matter the age, will always be little boys, always competing to show whose is bigger. That made me giggle at the time. Not so much now.

"So, Nathan will probably be out there for a while," I said out loud sounding disapprovingly a lot like little Frances, who was a wilting lily on the screen.

"Probably, had plans?"

"Kind of." I did, or make that, we did. We had carefully constructed plans, and he knew it. I told him I had something special I wanted to show him tonight. The fact he hadn't returned home yet burned a little. There was still time before dawn. So, I couldn't lose complete faith in him. But that faith was waning. I expected him to be waiting for me when I got back. Not out with the others. I felt an urge to slap my selfishness right out of me. Where it came from, I had to chalk it up as that more mature voice that often crept in and told me when to keep my mouth shut and when not to. Not that it spoke often, and sometimes when it did, it was nothing more than an easy to ignore whisper. It was good for Nathan to be out with the others, and I needed to trust my boyfriend. He knew we had plans and would be back. He hadn't ever let me down before. All I could do was sit and wait, and watch this show that I was starting to become rather involved in.

Would she and her beloved be allowed to be together? Forbidden love, the story as old as time, and something I knew a little bit about. I doubted Frances was the type of girl to break all the rules to be with him, like I had. I also doubted she would be the type to hop in the shower with him. What had occurred this morning was never far from my mind. How could it be? The feelings and sparks I felt were intoxicating. It made me wonder, and I just happened to be sitting next to someone that might be able to provide me a few answers.

"Laura, I have a question... and it's kind of a personal one."

"Okay, what is it?"

"Did you ever, you know, do something before you became a vampire and then found it was more intense after you became one?"

"You mean sex?" she asked directly.

"Mmm hmm." Maybe it was the time I grew up in that made me such a prude that I even had a hard time acknowledging that was what I was asking about.

"Oh yes," she replied without so much as even a glance away from the television. "Night and day. And not just any day. Christmas day. Your birthday. Halloween. Name any other special day. It is like that. And don't worry, it doesn't diminish, ever. It only gets better as you learn to let yourself go more." She leaned over next to me. "Just enjoy. It only gets better from here."

It gets better? It was going to get better? I wasn't sure I could handle that. What I had already experienced had blown my mind, and as it would seem, caused me to lose a little control.

"So, you never had it before?" asked Laura.

"No," I answered in a rush. "Remember, I was only sixteen."

"So?"

"Times were different," I said, then I pointed up at the screen. "They were more like those times."

"What times?" asked Marie. She was standing in the arched doorway with Jen and Kevin Bolden.

"What are you two talking about?"

"Oh nothing," I quickly answered, and even caught myself straightening up a little.

"Just girl talk while we watch this movie," added Laura.

Marie moved around so she could see the screen. "Oh, I love these old movies. Mind if I watch with you guys?"

"Not at all," replied Laura. "The more the merrier."

Marie took a seat on the chair to our right and settled in.

A movie night sounded good and reminded me of what we used to do up on the roof in the coven. I had other plans, and a participant in those plans was missing. "Jen, do you know when Nathan is coming back?"

She looked at Kevin awkwardly before answering. "Sorry, Larissa. I don't. He, Mike, Clay, and Marteggo went off somewhere a little while ago. I haven't seen them since."

That faith that was waning took a little more of a hit.

"Don't worry Larissa. I'm sure he is fine," Marie said in what was an obvious attempt to comfort me. "The guys and Theodora won't let anything happen to him. Remember, worry brings stress, and right now you don't need any of that." She reached over from the chair and rubbed my belly. "How are you feeling?"

Before I could answer, Laura popped off the sofa with a huff and stormed out of the room. Prompting an odd look from Jen and Kevin as she passed them and left out the front door.

13

The sun came up and Nathan still hadn't returned. I meandered downstairs to the kitchen and took the opportunity to spend some time with Amy while she ate breakfast. Steve and Stan had taken over her care in what I viewed as an understandable, albeit hostile takeover. There were benefits to the change. Amy and Cynthia seemed to have become closer. Both girls were the same age, and as they sat there at the table, one next to the other, they appeared to have their own language, made up of looks and hand motions. Which worked fine. It allowed them to communicate while Cynthia ignored my existence like she usually did.

I missed my time with Amy, and my heart melted sitting there while she ate cereal, and I munched on some dry toast. Why had I picked it up and tried it? I didn't know. After it didn't repulse me, I tried some more. A sight that caused that little girl giggle from Amy and more than a curious look from Stan, who was not hovering, but was still there with us. Cynthia, again, could have cared less. Stan was a little easier to talk to today than the last time I tried. I explained I could protect Amy, and he said he didn't disagree. He was concerned the others couldn't do the same when I wasn't around. I didn't have an answer for that, but there were two people in the house I could teach to take up some of the slack.

His friendly demeanor changed when Nathan walked down the hall past the door. Amy's did too, but she didn't go on the defensive like her older counterpart. She was still afraid, and I reached over to grab her hand to comfort her. In the corner of my eye, I saw Stan jerk in our direction, and I looked right at him.

"Sorry, my bad," he apologized.

It almost was bad. Not that I would have attacked him right there in front of Amy if he made the mistake of trying to separate me from her, but there would be a time later that I let my feelings out.

"Stay here with Stan and Cynthia," I said and kissed Amy on the forehead before I ran out the door, or tried. Her grip on my hand was as strong as mine, and it yanked me to a stop. I bent down and kissed her again. "I promise. You and I will spend some time together today, okay?" My eyes looked up over her head and directed the question to Stan, who just nodded. Amy eagerly agreed and let go of my hand.

"I have some training"—my hands made air quotes– "with the witches today. Would it be okay if she came along?" Amy spun around and looked at Stan. He was already smiling and just gave me a wave of his hand.

"I'll be back," I said, and this time I made it through the door in search of my boyfriend, who was hours late. It was easy to find him. All I had to do was follow the noise. They were back in the library talking loudly. Just in a few seconds, I heard the name Marteggo more than a few times. Seven, to be exact, but who was counting.

The secret door in the bookcase was open, and Jack was inside at the desk with a journal open. It was a common place to find him lately. Master Thomas was normally in there instructing him, but this morning he was nowhere to be found. I knew I needed to spend more time in there studying as well. It was the promise I made myself to continue my father's work, but before I could, I needed to catch up with him.

I stopped in the middle of the room, between the sofa and the coffee table, and this brought the rambunctious proceedings to a stop. You could have heard a pin drop in the library. As proof of that, I could hear Jack turning the pages of my father's journals.

"Nice of you to come back," I said, glaring right at Nathan.

I heard Mike chuckle from the chair he lounged in. Jeremy, Clay, and Brad stayed frozen where they were. Their eyes raced back and forth between each other. A brief spark from my fingers brought Mike back in line.

"We had plans," I said, and then added. "Important plans."

"I'm sorry. I guess we lost track of the time."

"Lost track of time?" I asked, my voice verged on a yell, but I held it back and under control. No matter how infuriating the stupid grin on Nathan's face made me feel. This was not that smile that melted me. Not that smile that made my brain stop working. This was one of those what-are-you-bugging-about-we-were-having-a-good-time smiles. Not one Nathan had ever shown before. It was something more common on Mike's mug. "We had plans. You were outside. Lost track of time? There is this great big ball light in the sky that comes up during the morning and goes down at night. How can you lose track of the time?"

"Relax Larissa. It's a little overcast. The sun wasn't too bad," replied Mike.

I turned and faced Mike. My control was teetering, and a small glow emanated from both of my hands. I heard the room clear behind me. Mike sat up in the chair and pushed back as far as he could get to add some distance between us. "Nathan and I had plans. Stay out of it." A tad bit of the piss and vinegar had made it into my tone, and it rubbed hard enough on Mike that he followed the rest out of the room, but circled around me as far as he could.

"We can go do whatever you wanted to do now. Like Mike said, the sun's not that bright, and he said it really isn't much more than a tickle when it hits you."

"First, for your education newbie, it is more than a tickle. Ask Marie who spent months locked in Jean's dungeon with the sunlight focused on her as torture. It's why we only went out when it was cloudy at the coven, and before you remind me of the times you and I went out to the cove or walked around in full sunlight, remember I am a witch. You shouldn't forget that, like ever." I caught myself and made myself take a moment to calm down before I sounded too much like something that rhymed with witch. "Second, we can't just go do whatever I wanted to do,"–sparks flew from my fingers as I added the air quotes–"last night right now. This was a special spot that I used to go out to at night when I was younger. I wanted to show it to you."

Nathan dropped that stupid grin from his face. "Sorry, we can go right now."

I crossed my arms, forgetting to stop the sparks in my fingers and giving myself a little jolt. I did my best to hide it and covered by thrusting them down in frustration. "No, it's not the same during the day."

He stood up and walked over to me. Ignoring the heat and energy flowing through my hands, he grabbed them, and pinned them behind my back, and looked down into my eyes. "Then tonight. I'm all yours."

Behind those big black eyes, I could see the passion that was my boyfriend. The same I saw before, and I knew he was sorry. He knew he messed up. I knew that even before he leaned down to kiss me, but if there were questions left, they were gone when our lips touched. When he released me, we were no longer alone in the room. Jack was still in my father's study. But there was another presence in the doorway. One that drew Nathan's attention a little quickly for my comfort.

"Is everything all right? I heard yelling." Theodora asked while leaning on the door frame seductively, which I didn't even know you could do. I know I couldn't. Not like her. If I tried, I would look like a drunken sloth hanging on to the doorframe for support. Not her. She was there like a movie poster. One hand extended up to the top, her long legs angled out toward the other side of the door, with the slit in her skirt riding high on her hip. Nathan's eyes took it all in.

"Everything's fine," I said as I pulled back from Nathan, but I kept a firm hold on his hand. A reminder for both Nathan and Theodora.

"No, it's not," said Nathan. I turned my head toward him in shock. Things were fine. We just made up, and I was letting him off the hook. What the hell was he talking about? "I messed up and missed plans that Larissa and I had last night."

"Well, that's okay," dismissed Theodora, which the words and her dismissive tone rubbed me the wrong way. "You guys have eternity together, Nathan. Don't sweat the small stuff. Now are you coming?"

Maybe I should be relieved that Nathan looked at me first before answering, but seeing he didn't explain or ask, I wasn't. He just turned back to her and answered, "yep," and bolted for the door.

"Wait!" I cried. "Where are you going now?"

"Marteggo invited us to come back. There is someone he wants us to meet," replied Nathan. Then it looked like a lightning bolt hit him in the head. He offered, "You should come too. It would be good for you to spend some time out there with the others."

"Yes, Larissa. Marteggo is very interested in getting to know you better."

I looked up at the clock on the wall and ducked my head. "I can't. I have training to do."

"More witch stuff?" Nathan asked.

"Yes, with Master Thomas and Marcus Meridian."

There was a gasp, and it wasn't from Nathan, or even Jack. Though if it came from the room behind me, it would have been understandable. Jack would have known the family name like I did. Everyone in our world should.

"Marcus is here?" asked Theodora.

"Yes, he is out there in the camp. Why? Do you know him?"

"We do," was all Theodora said, and she attempted to change the topic all together. "Let's not keep Marteggo waiting." She reached out and guided Nathan by the shoulder out the door with a lingering look back at me. "Larissa, don't forget you are a vampire. You should be with your own kind." Then she turned, and I watched as her hand ran down Nathan's back. If it had stayed there, she was going to meet my witch side in a way she would not forget.

"What was that about?" asked Jack.

"No clue, but I don't like it."

"She's something else."

I just rolled my eyes and stormed out, leaving Jack with a "Not you too."

14

"I promise I will watch after her."

Stan's over protectiveness around Amy grated on me. When we were at the coven, he barely acted like she even existed. She was always with me, and other than Ms. Parrish, not a soul had any concerns about it. "What's the worst that can happen? It's all witches, and she spent how long surrounded by them in the coven?"

There was no reply or objection from Stan as Amy took my hand and skipped enthusiastically down the hall behind me. It was a cool day outside. A strong breeze added to the chill. We stopped upstairs first to make sure she was properly dressed, not that she had an extensive wardrobe here. None of us did, and especially not with winter clothes. Us vampires didn't care. We were never hot or cold. An advantage. The same with Rob and Martin. Well, they were always hot, a benefit of who they were. It could be freezing outside, and they would be out in shorts. Shapeshifters and witches weren't so lucky. So, I made do. I imagined a few cute outfits and jackets and made sure they would be in the closet when we arrived upstairs. My own heart felt warm when I saw her all dressed in cute white leggings, boots, and a coat with fur around the collar. We took a moment to pose in front of the mirror, and I took a moment to suck in my gut. It didn't work.

Amy was more eager to be out around the witches than I was. She practically dragged me down the stairs. It took all I had to throw on the brakes at the door to the parlor, where I saw something unexpected. I believed all the vampires had left for more fun with Marteggo. A name that if I heard again, I might just vomit. Sitting there, like some sitcom scene, was the feminine contingent of our little group, minus Theodora, of course. She would undoubtedly be at her mate's side. "I thought you would be out with the others."

Laura was the first to break her gaze from the television. "Too much testosterone. There is only so much of Mike embarrassing himself I can take."

"Where are you two off to?" asked Jen.

"We are off to see–" I caught myself singing it as if we were about to skip down some yellow brick road. "I have more witchcraft training, and Amy wanted to come along."

"There's more to learn?" Laura asked with a tilt of her head.

"More than anyone can imagine," I replied and sighed.

She got the point and smiled. "Well, there might be more you need to learn about vampires, too."

I restrained a snarl in her direction. Yes, it was something I had always worried about, but this wasn't the right time for it to be thrown in my face. The solution to all of our problems was on the witch side. If it meant my vampire friends felt a little slighted by my showing favorites, then that was how it would have to be. In the end, they will see why.

"I'm curious," Marie said as she sprung up. "Care if I tag along?"

Well now, that was a curious proposition. I wouldn't mind showing Marie my other side. She only knew the vampire me, and never really saw the witch me. The presence of my vampire half in the witch camp already drew enough odd looks. Having her walk through it might push things a bit. Of course, there was a solution.

"Come along, but first, we need to make an adjustment." I raised my hand.

"Wait! Let me!" Lisa bounded down the stairs and went right up to Marie. Without hesitation, she raised her hand, and a golden glitter covered the woman. When it cleared, there was a pink hue to her skin, and an unfamiliar thumping in her chest.

"Nice!" I gave her a high-five.

"I'm coming too. I like it out there."

"You would," remarked Apryl.

I ignored her, chalking it up as just more sour grapes.

"The more the merrier." I reached back and ushered Lisa to join us before she responded to Apryl's comments. There was no sense in letting Lisa get pulled in and struck with any crossfire from the barbs aimed at me.

The four of us headed out. Amy held my hand the entire time. Lisa was on her other side. Out of the corner of my eye, I could see the little girl sneak a few glimpses up at Lisa. She wasn't afraid of her, and they had been around each other a lot, but I have to imagine her dark appearance might be a tad offsetting to young kids. It wasn't an accurate depiction of what she was truly like. Lisa was a sweetheart, and one of a few who I think actually understood me. It was more than just we had both ascended recently. We are both looked at oddly for who we are, or who part of us was. My being half vampire and witch, and she, a witch but, of the dark magic variety, who talks and plays with dead things variety. Slowly, Amy reached up with her other hand and grabbed hold of Lisa's hand.

Closer to the camp, I glanced out at the edge of the woods. I couldn't see anyone particular out in the open, but I knew they were there. I knew for sure there were five somewhere out among the trees.

The sight of the dozens of tents of various colors and the columns of smoke rising from campfires drew Amy's attention. She pulled hard on my arm, wanting to reach the camp faster. As we entered, I watched to see if anyone took any notice of Marie, and they didn't. They still took notice of me. There was no doubt about that.

"What's in the pots?" Marie asked.

Most of the campfires had pots suspended over them on metal frames or makeshift wooden ones. Inside, something boiled.

"Eyes of newt, and frogs' ears," answered Lisa, and she did so with a straight face and tone. A feat I would have struggled to pull off.

"Really?" Amy asked, and hearing the curiosity and wonderment in her voice, I felt guilty for not cutting Lisa's little joke off before it went too far.

"No, not really. It's just their breakfast."

I heard the sigh of disappointment come from Amy. Even though she spent a lot of time around us, I believed she still had this fantasy image of what we were.

"Plus, frogs don't have ears."

"Spoiled-sport," objected Lisa.

I didn't care. I wanted to show Amy and Marie what it was truly like, and a realistic view of witches was what they were going to get. That in itself will be magical enough.

"So, are we meeting Marcus Meridian?"

"Not sure Lisa. He might be there, but he might not. We are going up here, to the yellow tent, to see James O'Conner. He is going to teach me how to see the future."

"Divination?" asked Lisa. I wondered if I was the only witch that didn't know that word.

"Yes, that."

"Why would you…" Lisa clamped her mouth shut and let go of Amy's hand. She spun around in front of me and took a few steps backwards before stopping and forcing me to stop before I ran her over. "You aren't…," she started, stuttering her way through both words. "The seven…"

"Stop," I said, and slammed my hand over her mouth. I shook my head, but her eyes widened, and I felt a grin growing under my hand. "Just stop." I released my grip. "I'm just learning new skills. That is all. We should never stop learning. Isn't that what Mrs. Saxon said once?" I wasn't sure if she had or not, but it sure sounded like something she would have.

Lisa's grin turned into a quirky, lopsided smirk. She wasn't buying it. I knew her well enough to know that, but I also knew her well enough to know she was going to drop it. When we were alone, this would become a game of twenty, or more, questions. I grabbed her shoulders and turned her around. "You know, James is kind of cute." Then I gave her a little shove. That was all it took for Lisa to lead the way up to his tent. She didn't even pause at the opening, and marched right in.

I ducked through the opening with Amy and Marie. Our first meeting was outside, not inside in his tent. I didn't really know what to expect, but I definitely didn't expect an apartment overlooking a bar on Bourbon Street in downtown New Orleans. The combination of old southern brick walls and wide plank pine floors and industrial metal railings and accents was both stunning and beautiful. I took a few notes for my use later. It might be time to update the farmhouse, which would be as easy as a snap.

"You came, and you brought friends." James announced as he came down the stairs that I guessed led up to his bedroom. There were no obvious sleeping quarters in the open floor plan room we were in. His kitchen was tucked against the far wall, and a large spacious living area in front of the wall of windows that overlooked party central below.

"I did," I said, as he walked right past Lisa, creating a scowl. "This is Amy O'Neil, and Marie Norton."

He bent down to Amy. "It's very nice to meet you Amy. You ready to be a big sister?"

Amy giggled. Lisa gasped, and I about died. "Did Marcus tell you?"

"Nope, you will in a few days. Now you don't need to." He grinned, and held up his hands, and pushed up his sleeves, showing there were no tricks up them. "And I know all about Amy, and completely understand the situation. Something else you will explain to me when I make a similar comment. It is an easy assumption for people to make, with how you feel about her and all."

I pulled Amy close, not to protect her from James, but because he was right. I felt so deeply for that girl, like she was my own.

"It is fascinating to me. She must have learned and picked up that caring trait from you." He turned to Marie. "You did the same thing so many years ago and raised a wonderful woman. The world thanks you." He bowed and took her hand.

This could become tiring.

He then stood up and turned toward Lisa. "Hi Lisa. Don't worry. We have a pleasant conversation in two days, and I have already decided I don't mind teaching you too." Lisa looked back at him as confused as I felt, and he just cracked that wide smile again.

"So," he turned back and clasped his hands, and stretched them in front of him, cracking his knuckles. "Shall we get to it? But wait, there is something we need to take care of first." He bent back down to Amy. "It appears you have something in your ear."

I watched as his hands flashed around in front of Amy, and he palmed a quarter before he slipped his hand by her ear. His other hand pointed up at me. "Don't ruin it for her."

I stepped back.

"How are you going to hear all this Amy, with this in your ear?" He pulled out the quarter, just like birthday magicians had done for years, but that didn't matter.

She still looked at his hand in awe, even after all the magic she had seen. Then the quarter fell, and another twenty followed it before disappearing onto the floor. He was showing off. I just wasn't sure for who.

"All right. Let's get to it." He hopped up. "Divination, or what others call, the art of future telling. First, you don't need a crystal ball or anything. None of those fortune tellers really can see anything. The crystal ball is just a distraction. I call them fortune guessers. Ask a few questions and watch the reaction. Then they build on it. Knowing about future events, or things that are more random, is where the trick is, and that is what I am going to show you, but I need you to put something in your mind. It won't make a lot of sense to you right now, but one day it will. Time is not a when, it's a where. No one can truly travel into the future, but some of us can see far enough down the road in front of us to see what is coming. Does that make sense?"

"Sure," I said with a head full of scrambled eggs.

"Come, let's have a seat while I explain. First, can I get you anything? Amy? Lisa? Would either of you like something to drink.?" His refrigerator popped open, showing a wide assortment of sodas and juices. "Help yourselves. Larissa, I'm not sure what you and Marie may like, but feel free to conjure whatever it is that would be."

"Wait? You know what Marie is?" Lisa asked, as she examined the options for her and Amy.

"Yep, but relax, not many will be able to see through it. I can see it because I saw when you did it, and I can see when you will remove it."

"Huh," I remarked and had a seat on the black leather sofa and admired the view outside the windows. James sat on the front edge of a matching lounge chair positioned catty cornered to my right. "I'm serious. Stop thinking of time as the hands on a clock going around. It's not a when, it's a where. Think of a road. You can look back and see where you just came from. What is right behind you is easier to see, thus it is easier to remember. What is way back there, miles away, is just a spot in the haze on that hot summer day and is harder to see, and your memories are less clear. That is, unless something happened at that spot. Like you visited an amusement park or something. That spot is a little bigger, with more signs reminding you of its location, so those memories stick with you longer. It's the same with looking forward. You can see what is coming ahead of you, but the difference is, when you are looking back, you have been there. You won't actually be at that spot ahead of you until you get there, but that doesn't mean you can't see it. Does that make sense?"

That was both a big *hell no*, and a *hell yeah*, which only added to the spin in my head. It was a simple explanation for one of the most complex problems in the world. Not even Einstein could explain time, but this was magic, not science, and those laws didn't apply here. Here, there were no laws. Now the question was, how to take what he just explained and use it. "I guess. I mean, I get it, but I don't understand what to do with it. Is there a spell or something?"

"Nah, nothing that fancy." He sat back and looked to be in thought. "Have you ever had hunches about something, and then found out you were right?"

"We all do," I answered. What he just described was human nature.

He exploded forward in his seat and leaned as close to me as he could, bracing his arms on his legs. "No, we all think we do, but we don't. Yes, everyone has hunches, or gut feelings as they are called, but they are rarely right. What I am talking about is hunches that are mostly, or always right. They may even be something you dismiss. I need you to think. Have you ever noticed that? This is important."

"Maybe. I don't know."

"Think back. This part is important." Then his arm jerked up and pointed a single finger at Lisa.

"I have," spouted Lisa. "I've had visions and feelings that have come true. Not often, but I've had them."

James got up and walked over to the lounge chair Lisa sat in. "I know, and as we will talk about in a few days, your grandmother exposed you to this practice many years ago. She would use tea leaves and auto-writing to view events yet to come, but you found another way that is easier. Which it is. Using something like Celtic runes and bones, are just magnifiers. It is better if you learn how to do this without."

"James, won't all this telling me about what we will talk about in a few days, change what we talk about?" asked Lisa. It was a good question, and one I had wondered about earlier when he preempted all of my introductions.

"Not at all. I'm careful about what I expose to avoid changing the natural flow of the world. I use this gift to observe, and not to manipulate. It would be irresponsible to do anything else." From the center of the floor, he stood and looked at us both. "Here is the first instruction. I need you to clear your mind. A cluttered mind clogs up the senses. If you need to do some kind of meditation, do it. Some cultures use substances as part of a ritual just to clear one's mind, but I prefer not doing that. This needs to be something you learn how to do at a moment's notice so you can use it when needed." He took a deep breath, raised his hands up to shoulder height and then slowly pressed them down to his side as he let it out. "Clear your mind. Now try it."

"Try what?" I asked, still unclear about what he was describing. Okay, clear my mind, and then what? Clearing my mind would not be a trivial act as it was. It was going to be an impossible act if I was sitting here wondering what the next step was.

"Just close your eyes."

"All right," I said, and then watched Lisa as she sat there in what looked like complete peace. Oh, I was so jealous.

"Larissa, close your eyes." I must have been a little too slow for his taste. Imagine that. Me being too slow at anything. I closed them. "Now clear your mind. After that I will tell you what to do next. Trust me, this will work. I've already seen it."

A simple, but impossible task with my mind still focused on what was next. How to clear it was also cluttering it up. I was the true portrait of irony. It took a bit, but I fought against the thoughts of what was next, and won. With that out, I felt a little more relaxed. My mind was clearer, but not completely clear. There was too much going on in my world to actually be vacant of all thoughts.

"Okay, I'm ready," reported Lisa. My natural sarcasm called Lisa a showoff, further clouding my thoughts.

"Just a few more moments. Still giving Larissa a little more time before I give her a booster shot."

"A what?" I demanded. My eyes opened in enough time to see James's thumb hitting me on the forehead, and then everything went black and my mind was clear.

"Now, imagine you are standing on that road. Where you are standing is here in this apartment with all of us. Just behind you are the moments when you sat down, walked in through the door, and even just a little further back than that is when left your home to come here. Each of those are clear as they just happened. Things that happened last week, not so much. Do you see the road?"

"Yes," answered Lisa.

"What about you Larissa? Do you see it?"

"I guess," I answered knowing full well I didn't.

"Larissa, open your eyes and look at me."

I did what James directed and opened my eyes and looked right at him. His face was just a foot or so away from mine. His kind eyes reached out to me. "This is not some imaginary or metaphysical road. This is one of the few times us witches can be literal, like the runes. Imagine an actual road. It can be any road. Straight. Winding. What ever kind of road you want." He reached out and grabbed my head gently. "Now close your eyes again, and imagine that road."

I did, and imagined a long straight road that cut across open fields. It disappeared off into the distance ahead of me. I turned and looked back and it did the same in that direction.

"Got it?" asked James.

"Good. Now look ahead of you. Out there lies every event that hasn't happened yet. Every milestone of your life and the lives of those you know are out there. Think of one. See if it will come to you, but try to not be too eager. Pick something close. Something right there in front of you."

The clutter returned to my head, but instead of crowding out what I was trying to do, event after event bounced around, wanting attention. I just needed to pick one. Which would I choose? My baby? My future with Nathan? As I ran through them, there was one that shadowed over all other questions. Its shadow loomed over my entire future. I thought about it, and all other thoughts cleared, except that one. Excitement built inside me. The possibility of finding an answer, of clearing this cloud away from my path, was almost too much to contain. But even with all that focus, my head was full of a black nothingness, and this wasn't some magical realm or potion created space like Mrs. Tenderschott took me too. This was the emptiness of my head coming up with a big fat nothing.

"All right Lisa. Keep it to yourself. Larissa needs some more time."

"You know I can hear you," I reminded him.

"I know. I also know how much longer it is going to take for you to get it." He said, his voice was close to me. Almost right in my face. I opened my eyes. "Don't open your eyes or the world will come crashing down around you." I slammed them shut before I saw how close he was. "You hold the fabric of the world in your hand." His voice boomed all around me.

I felt my body tense up and wished he had told us this before we started. Having that kind of responsibility might have been something I would have passed on.

"Just kidding," he laughed. "But I don't want you to lose the frame of mind you are in."

My body relaxed, and I stuck my tongue out at him, keeping my frame of mind steady and clear.

"Also, maybe I should have told you to just sit and let something come to you. Or think of something really short. Like what I am holding in my arms when you finally open your eyes. Trying to focus on an event of your choosing is hard, especially one so far ahead. Remember the road analogy. From where you are right now, Larissa, you can't see the on ramp for that decision. There are hundreds of intersections to cross before you get there, all of which are also too far away to be within view."

I let my disappointment out with a huff. Yes, he should have mentioned that earlier. That would have saved me time and frustration, but I had noticed a lot of what I would call the witch-way involved frustration. Instead of telling you exactly how, it required you to struggle through a series of mistakes first, then you hit the jackpot. That feeling of accomplishment made the successes all the better and helped cement the lesson inside of you, and it worked. I could attest to that with so many examples, but that didn't mean I had to like the method.

"I am going to have you keep your eyes closed for another minute. Think about what you are going to see when you open them. A minute in the grand scheme of time is just in front of your toes on the road. Three minutes, a grain of sand further. It's not that far to look. If you focus, you can see it from here." His voice took on a melodic tone. "What did my apartment look like when you closed your eyes? What will it look like when you open them again? What will it look like in three minutes?"

I saw his apartment. The style I liked so much, and we were all there, just like we were when I closed my eyes. Was I seeing a memory or the future? It was hard to tell. Had anyone moved since I closed my eyes? If not, then this was the past, or was it? Maybe they had moved, which made what I saw the future, or maybe I saw them where they were earlier before the moment I closed my eyes, which would be the past. It required a lot of that term I couldn't stand, focus. You had to remember all the details and then compare. It reminded me of an activity book Edward once pointed out that Amy would like. It was full of pictures. After looking at one picture, you flipped the page and tried to identify all the differences in this version of the picture. I scanned around the image in my head. Nothing seemed to be different. I looked back to the side. Coming in and out of focus. There was something on the couch next to me that wasn't there before. I opened my eyes and looked right at the spot between me and Amy. It was empty.

Confused, I looked up at James. "Just wait, and that confused feeling will eventually go away." He pointed back at the spot on the sofa. I watched, as did everyone else in the room.

"Give it another half a minute," said Lisa. "I saw the clock."

"What clock?" I asked.

Lisa pointed up to the digital clock on the table behind the sofa. Its big blue neon numbers said it was 11:07 AM. I hadn't looked up that far in my vision, but I was now. I watched as the ':' flashed on and off, denoting the ticking seconds. To my left, Lisa was whispering a countdown.

"Three. Two. One."

Right on cue, a black cat hopped up on the table and then down on to the sofa, and curled up next to me.

"Oh, a cat," cooed Amy. She reached over tentatively.

"Don't worry. Archimedes doesn't bite. He likes to be scratched between the ears."

I leaned back and pointed, while Amy gave him a good scratching. The cat leaned into her hand, wanting more. "You conjured that there, didn't you?"

"Nope. Archimedes is a real honest to God cat, and before you suggest the next question, I know you are going to ask, did I cause him to hop up there through some training? Try training a cat and tell me how that goes. What you saw was just a few moments into the future. By the time we are done, you will be able to see quite a ways into the future, and it won't be a struggle. It will take work, I already know that, but you will get it. Just trust and do what I am saying. Can you do that?"

I reached over and gave Archimedes a scratch. At first, he acted leery of my touch. It was probably the coolness in my fingers, but after he felt the scratching, he acted like he didn't care anymore.

"Remember, you have nothing to lose. I have already seen the outcome." He raised his eyebrows up and gave me a goofy grin.

"All right, you're on." I agreed.

"That's great. Now you two have the gift, but you will never be as cool as me. I see everything a few seconds, minutes, or even days before it happens."

"That sounds like a headache," commented Lisa.

"It is until you learn how to filter things. Then it's an advantage. No matter what it is, you see it coming."

"Did you see Larissa coming?" Lisa asked.

"Or me?" piped in Amy.

"Oh, absolutely little girl. I knew an adorable little girl was coming. Cuteness glows red in my visions." He winked in my direction. "I knew something was coming. I didn't know what it was, but I had visions of Jean retreating in fear, and others coming out of the shadows. Not all my visions are crystal clear. Some are just flashes. Some are full conversations. You have to learn how to save them and pull all the details you can from them. Let's try again."

"Okay," I agreed.

James looked at Lisa for an agreement, and I had to wonder why he did. If what he just said was true, he already knew what her answer would be. Then, remembering back to the crazy introduction session we had when we arrived, I understood. As unnerving and messy as it might be for him to see the world that way, it would be even worse for those around him. Imagine interacting with someone who was always several steps ahead of you. I imagine trust wouldn't be that high. So, he must be going through the motions for everyone else's comfort.

"I'm game," added Lisa.

"Now this time, Larissa, don't think of a question like you did before. Just let it flow and tell me what you see. I will help you to interpret those visions. Lisa, just do what you did last time."

Over the next several hours, Marie and Amy kept Archimedes busy, or vice versa. There was a lot of giggling in the background. Marie made Amy some lunch, with James's help. All of this happened while Lisa and I played a magical game of red car, blue car. We sat at the window trying to predict what cars would drive down the road at various points in the future. We started with shorter time intervals, and then progressed to ten minutes, twenty minutes, and then multiple cars over thirty-minute intervals. James said this was a game he played with himself to refine his skill. Then he started working on predicting every person who would walk into the bar across the street and when, hours before they even arrived.

His routine for training started every day at noon. He would sit at the window and focus on that night writing down the description of everyone he saw and logging when they would arrive using the time shown on the same clock Lisa had used to tag when Archimedes would appear. He explained that the list, at times, would be as long as several hundred people, with full descriptions of what they were wearing, if they arrived alone or with someone, and if they left alone or with someone. Even how two strangers would have paired up before they left. If some of his visions were longer about a particular person, he would actually go down and sit at the bar to watch and see how much of what he saw was correct.

To me this sounded like perfecting an ability, but then James put the cherry on top, and explained he had stretched it to something that happened several months into the future, eight months being the furthest. Of course, referring back to his road example, what he could see wasn't all that clear and precise. More of a feeling and some fleeting details that he could put together over the next several months.

"Now just pick your method for testing yourself daily. It's like a muscle. You have to use it to strengthen it."

"We could pick who is going to drool on the floor first, Rob or Martin?"

Amy laughed at Lisa's proposal, and James appeared to be confused. It was nice to see the shoe on the other foot, but I let him off and explained, "Werewolves."

"Ah. Stop by in two days and we will work on it again together."

"Will do," responded Lisa and she helped gather up Amy so we could leave. Amy had chased the cat upstairs a little while ago.

"Now, Larissa, you have a question you are going to ask me."

"I do?" I asked, unsure of what he was referring to.

"See, you did." He chuckled, humored at himself. Being the butt of what I felt was an ill delivered joke didn't amuse me. "But that wasn't it. Earlier you were trying to see how all this ends up for you. Don't try. You can't see your own future like that. You can see those that are around you and might infer what happens to you from them, but you can't see your own future. You are just observing that point. Remember, you haven't really been there, but you can see what is out there."

"Wait." That didn't make any sense to me. "If I am there observing, then I am there."

"No," he shook his head. "You aren't there. You are here, looking at that spot through a huge telescope. Don't force it to make sense right now. The more you do it, the more sense it makes. Especially once you start to see what I call the conversations."

"Okay, I'll have to trust you on that," I conceded, reluctantly. "I have one last question." I was very hesitant to ask. Hearing that I couldn't see my own future was a hard buzz kill to the question that drove me earlier. It explained the big empty nothingness I found when I searched for that moment in time. It was also possible I just wasn't skilled enough, or unable, to see that far yet. Either was possible, but James gave me another avenue, or angle to explore. Lisa probably wasn't there yet. She was learning this skill with me, but James was an expert.

"Go on."

"Shouldn't you already know?" I sniped back, trying to cover the nerves around what I was about to ask.

"Well, we could play it two ways. I could tell you I do and give you the response without you ever asking, or you could ask, and I tell you the same thing. Which would make you feel better?" I expected to see his signature Cheshire cat type grin that carried an annoying level of arrogance, but I didn't. This was serious James, and it was the first time I had seen this side of him. I didn't much like it.

"I'm okay with either," I said, trying to pull his jovial nature back to the surface.

"Marie, can you take Amy out into the hall for just a moment? I need to talk to Larissa and Lisa privately."

I failed. I completely failed. The room felt like it grew colder, though it probably hadn't. I wouldn't know if it really had. It had definitely become darker, and that had nothing to do with the sun going down outside. Lisa even looked like she felt it. She sat back down slowly, with her hands tightly clasped on her lap.

"Most cannot do this. Lisa, it is part of the dark arts, so it makes more sense for you to have this ability. Larissa, it's probably a family trait. You both need to realize this is a gift, and it shouldn't be abused. Don't use it to manipulate anyone, human or witch. That should go without saying, and that is not the most important warning. You need to be careful what you try to look at with your gift. You might not like the answer you find. Which is why you should never attempt to find out about your own future, or ask anyone else to tell you. Imagine if you found out the worst news you could think of, but there was nothing you could do about it from that day until the day it happens. That is a true hell that has caused many a witch to live a tortured life. Divination should never be used selfishly. During the test of the seven wonders, the why you use it is as important as the ability."

He stepped forward and offered me his hand. I took it and he pulled me out of that hole the weight of his words plunged me into. I swear I felt a shake in my knees as I stood there.

"Do I know your future?" he asked out loud. "I know bits and pieces of both of your futures, but that is my gift, and scar to bear, and I will not tell you or anyone anything about it. Your destiny is not as important as the journey you will travel to get there."

15

"Oh, my word! You guys should have seen Larissa today," Marie gushed with all the pride of a proud parent. I wasn't really sure why though, and why she cheered every time either Lisa or I made a correct read. Yes, those reads were impressive to us because we knew what it meant, but I had to imagine from the outside it was a rather boring show. Two girls sitting there with their eyes closed, calling out various claims waiting to find out if we were correct or not. I imagined she would be more awestruck by balls of fire flying across the land at one another, or something appearing from nothing. I made a note to show her some of that one day. That would give her something to truly gush over.

"Did she set a dresser on fire?" mocked Apryl. "You know she did that once. Remember that Larissa?"

"Oh, I remember. I remember, but at least I didn't set you on fire."

Apryl responded with a single and loud, "Ha!"

The rest of the room basically ignored me, and at the moment, I was okay with that. I didn't need or want, to be the center of attention. That occurred far too often for my liking already, no fault of my own. And, if Marie planned to continue to retell our adventures of the day, she would have to do it without me. I had important and already once delayed plans, but first I had to kill two birds with one stone.

I walked over to Laura, who did her best to look around me until I blocked her view of the television. Behind me, I was sure there was some old movie playing. These seemed to be a source of fascination and bonding for Jen and Laura.

"Can you watch Amy for a bit? At least until Stan or Steve come to get her." I could have asked Lisa, Jack, or one of the werewolves to do this, but I remembered how the episode the other night with Nathan stung her.

"That won't mess up your perfect little family?" she asked. The question about knocked me over. I was trying to be nice.

"Laura, what's wrong?" I asked. Not really wanting to get into it in the middle of everyone, but she opened that door. I wasn't about to just shut it and lock away whatever issue she had behind it. It needed to come out.

"Nothing," she spat, and then held out her arms. "Amy, come sit with us. You'll like these flying monkeys."

Amy hesitated for a moment and held her place next to Lisa. Laura took notice, frowned, and then looked straight up at me with a lot of venom. I ignored her. We needed to hash out whatever this was, but I didn't have time now. This had to wait. "Amy, why don't you sit with Laura and watch this movie before dinner is ready?"

Lisa urged her forward. "Go on. I'm going to go help Jack cook. Hopefully it will be edible tonight."

Amy shuffled her feet slowly and when Laura reached out for her again, Amy appeared to relax and walked into her waiting arms, only pausing slightly to look up at me when she passed.

"I have something to do with Nathan tonight," I explained.

She looked back again, just before Laura picked her up and sat her between her and Jen Bolden. "What about story time?"

"Tomorrow, I promise. Plus, you don't want to miss this movie." I didn't know what the movie was, but it was old, and I was sure Amy had never seen it before.

"This is a classic," added Jen. "You'll love it. I first saw it when I was your age."

Marie walked into the room and looked at the screen. "Oh, I love this movie. Can I watch with you guys?" It was a rhetorical question she had directed at Amy, who nodded wildly and moved over to make room for Marie.

"Go," Jennifer Bolden mouthed in my direction, and I took the moment of distraction to leave before Amy noticed, but I wasn't fast enough.

Laura reached up and touched my belly, which now both looked and felt larger than I remembered from this morning. "Showing there a bit, aren't you?"

The entire room shifted its focus to me, including Amy. I backed away and left, longing for the protection of the hallway from the collective gaze that followed me and made me feel like a freak.

Lisa had already departed for the kitchen, and I could hear the sounds of something happening in there. There were a few smells wafting down the hall. I was thankful I didn't need to eat.

Waiting at the top of the stairs was who I was looking for, and I quickly crossed my arms across my stomach to hide our new growing addition.

"I'm present and accounted for. Ready?"

"Give me a minute. I want to change. Wait for me out on the porch, okay?"

Nathan reluctantly agreed and tried to embrace me once I reached the top of the stairs, but I spun around to avoid it.

"I will be ready in just a minute." I couldn't risk him seeing it, not yet. I was already using magic to keep him and the others from feeling its heartbeat. I wasn't sure if I did anything to hide my bump if I would harm the life within. If I was right, magic created this. How would it react to more? I didn't know.

My self-created wardrobe wasn't exactly what I needed for the occasion. Form fitting clothes meant to get and hold his attention were not what I needed at the moment. I needed to hide something, something that was bigger than this morning, and now strained against the waistband of my pants. Looser jeans were in order and soon appeared. Of course, they fit perfectly. How long they would continue to fit? Who knew? Theodora said vampire pregnancies were accelerated. Compared to other pregnant women I had seen, I believed I was now about two or three months along, even though it had only been three days. The last thing I threw on was something I had never worn before in my life. Hell, by morning I could be another month along. For some room to grow into, I pulled on a hoodie for the first time in my life. Hoodies weren't a thing when I was growing up, and since then, I didn't really wear anything baggy. I walked down the stairs looking more like Apryl than myself and hoped to slip past the door with no remarks.

If there were any comments, I didn't hear them. I was down the stairs and out the door in a flash. I grabbed Nathan's hand in full stride and yanked the poor boy off the porch. It took him a few steps before he caught his footing, but he soon joined me stride for stride as we headed around the house and passed the barn. We didn't stop there. We kept going across the field. My father would have freaked if he were alive and had seen us. We cut right through the old planting areas and didn't keep to the walkways he created. I felt Nathan slow down after we hit the trees. Probably a habit from all the trips he had made with the others recently. "Come on," I called, and gave him a good yank.

We kept going from what I knew was about half a mile. The destination was a place I knew well. Or I did a long time ago. I hadn't considered if it was still there after all these years, or if I could even find it. My directions were, head to this tree, and then to that tree. I was sure those trees had grown through the years, or may have even been knocked down by a storm. Could I even still find them? That was a big question.

To my surprise, I found the first tree with no issue. Then the second. The third was bigger, and leaned more than I remembered, but it was absolutely it, and I knew my destination was just a few feet away. Well, should have been just a few feet away. Now it was a few feet away, and a few feet up. A wide crook in an old Live Oak tree that made the perfect seat to just sit and listen to the river under the concert of crickets and frogs. To me, this was the most peaceful place in the world when I was a child. My father and I found it while out on our many walks, and he lifted me up and placed me where the trunk split into two, creating the perfect seat. I remember sitting there, with one leg draped down, leaning back against one large, towering branch. He would climb up and join me. Looking up at the spot now, I doubted he could climb up there now. Hell, I would have been a challenge for him to lift me up that high.

I pointed up and started my ascent. Which wasn't much more than a jump and a grab. Nathan stood there at the bottom of the tree and looked up. I motioned for him to follow and watched as he studied the tree. I guess he hadn't completely tested his limits yet. He was going for the more traditional attempt at climbing up. His shoes slipped on the bark each time he tried. I couldn't help laughing at his attempts, and that seemed to frustrate him. I thought he would have seen how I got up here, but he went back and again tried to climb the trunk, this time, trying to reach as far around the trunk as he could, which wasn't far. This tree was probably twelve to fifteen feet around.

"Don't be silly. Just jump up here," I suggested from high upon my perch.

"Jump?"

"Yes, jump. Like I did." I backed up to give him room to land.

It was now more than obvious he hadn't tried to jump as a vampire. He backed up and got a running start. Which was good for jumping a long way, but not for height. He found that out the hard way, smacking the trunk of the tree, sending a shudder up and through its limbs, before falling flat on the wet ground. Now I had to sit down. I was laughing so hard; I would have fallen over if I hadn't. Nathan slammed the ground with his fist before standing back up.

"Just stand there," I tried to suggest, but I was laughing too hard. I waved my hands around hysterically in front of myself, as if that would help me regain my composure. It didn't. At least not at first, but eventually I pulled myself together enough to lean down, offering a hand and suggested, "Just stand right there, and jump straight up. Trust me."

Nathan stood up and brushed off the leaves and dirt he gathered when he fell to the ground. He looked up reluctantly and then looked back at the tree.

"Come on," I encouraged.

He finally jumped, and didn't put his all into it either, coming up a few feet shorter than I expected. Luckily, I had my hand held out, and I caught him. I yanked him up the rest of the way and sat him against the large branch. I sat down next to him, and let my leg dangle off like I used to.

"So, this is your special place?" Nathan asked.

"Wait!" I held up a finger. "Just wait and listen."

I nuzzled next to him, and we just sat and listened. In the silence, there it was. An old familiar tune. The Mississippi River rolling down the river with a low roar. The crickets welcoming the coming night. It was more fantastic than I remembered. My new vampire hearing, that tool nature, or whatever created us, gave us to hunt, had opened the door, allowing new and subtle sounds to fill out the chorus. The rustling of leaves in the breeze, the clicking of barren branches.

"This is it," I whispered.

It didn't take long before Nathan got it. His eyes and ears chased every sound, and took it all in.

"My father and I found this spot when I was seven. We came out here often to just sit and listen. When I got older, I would come out here myself. I even snuck out of my room a few times late at night to come out here and look up at a full moon." I looked up through the branches, just hoping to find a sight of it, but a layer of clouds obscured my view. Only the glow of the celestial orb was visible. It was still magical without it, but I wanted, needed, this night to be perfect. I waved my hand across the sky and uttered two simple words from one of my father's journals, "Etre visible." It was French, which many of the spells in my father's journals were. The clouds parted and revealed the glorious moon behind it casting long shadows along the ground. Now it was all perfect.

"Nathan, I have something to tell you." My insides flopped around uncontrollably. I wrapped my arms around my stomach, hoping to hold things together long enough to tell him. My god, was I bigger?

"What is it?" he asked.

I caught a whiff of something on his breath. Like many a woman throughout the history of the humanity, I smelled a telltale smell that interrupted my train of thought and stopped our conversation right there. No, it wasn't the fragrance of another woman on his clothes. No, it wasn't the acidic or sweet smell of alcohol. If it were, I might have made a comment and let it go in the end. It wasn't all that important, and I didn't believe we could get drunk. One of our benefits. At least we couldn't get drunk off of alcohol. There was something we could become inebriated from and develop a strong and devastating addiction.

"Did you feed again today?" I sat up and peeled myself from Nathan's side.

"Yeah, why?"

"I can smell it on you. That's what, twice in three days?" This wasn't good. He was giving in to his urges. Kevin should have covered this.

Nathan held up three fingers.

"Three times?"

"Yep." He announced it proudly.

"You can't do it that often, Nathan. You need to develop control. If you don't, it will control you." Oh my god, I sank inside when I realized how much I sounded like Marie when she lectured me on the same topic. The difference, I hadn't fed three times in three days. I hadn't even fed twice in three days. It was just once a week at the most. At that point I had only fed once, ever, but her point was clear.

"Nah, it's fine. Marteggo said it is. He said it's how we gain our strength."

"Nathan." I turned toward him and held his face in my hands. "It is what gives us our strength, but if you feed too much, you are feeding the urges instead of learning how to control them. That will make it difficult or impossible to be around humans."

"So, what's the problem with that?"

"Plenty," I said, letting go of his face and backing up, doing everything but placing my hands on my hips. Not only couldn't I believe what he said, I couldn't believe how he said it. He was obstinate.

"Hello," I screamed leaning over him. "Wake up and smell the world. It's full of humans. People with a pulse. How are you going to learn to live with them if you are constantly wanting to feed off them?"

"Who says we have to?"

Well now, that was the five-year-old logic I expected from my boyfriend, not. I couldn't decide rather to scream the obvious at him, or slap him across the face until he realized how stupid that question was. My slaps might not feel like much to someone so well fed, and newly born, so I opted for another path. "Are you stupid or something? Are you feeding on slugs and snails or has your brain slowed down like that all on its own? The world is full of them. We can't really avoid them."

"But Marteggo says the best life is one with a little house out away from everyone. A place all our own, where we can be what we are and around others that are like us. He has lived that way for years now and loved it."

"A life of exile. That is what he has lived. Remember, they forced him out. Before that, he lived in New Orleans with everyone else." A part of the story that Nathan was conveniently forgetting at the moment.

"That's not how Marteggo described it."

Hearing that name made my skin crawl. I saw where this was going. A charismatic figure that everyone looked up to in the past, and some still did, described this beautiful freeing life to someone who had been a vampire all of three days. Just three days. What wasn't to like about the description of heaven? Even I had to admit there was an aspect to it I found wonderful. Thinking back to my life with the Nortons, that was basically how we lived. We were off, away from anyone, doing our own thing. About as far on the outskirts of town that one person could get before being in the next town, but even then, our paths crossed with others. We weren't completely isolated. Nathan had to realize that, or was Marteggo's glow blinding him?

"I don't care what Marteggo says. We...," I pointed back and forth between the two of us. "We need to learn to live in the world around us. Not isolated to just vampires. Remember, we have friends who are not vampires."

"Maybe we shouldn't," he said, and grinned sheepishly.

"What did you just say?" I asked, shocked that something so preposterous came out of my boyfriend's mouth.

"Maybe we should only be with other vampires."

"Might I remind you that you have several friends that are not. Rob. Martin. Remember them? Oh, and what about your mother, who I believe one day will be part of your life again?" Then I exploded on him, "What about Amy?" In reality I wasn't thinking about her. Well, I was, but I wasn't. I was thinking of the other child in our life. The newest child. The one I wasn't sure if they would be human, or vampire.

"I don't know," he confessed. I felt relieved. We were finally getting somewhere.

"See..." I started, hoping to bring him back around, but then he opened his mouth and blasted me right in the gut.

"Amy should be with Steve, Stan, and Cynthia. They are shifters like her."

That was it. I hopped down out of the tree and marched away from it. I just couldn't take anymore. My boyfriend. The man I thought I knew better than anyone. Someone I thought I knew well enough to know what he was going to say before he ever opened his mouth was different now. Yes, he had been turned into a vampire, which was my fault. That was the physical change, and that was heartbreaking enough. But I thought that was where it stopped, and had even looked at this change as a positive. Well, not entirely, but it had its good parts. He would never age. He would never get sick. He would never die. When, and I hoped, there was a point we would, we finally said 'til death do us part, it truly meant we would be together forever. I never expected to lose the best of him. The strong and compassionate person he was.

I looked back in the tree's direction as the first tear rolled down my cheek. I was too devastated to laugh at the sight of him trying to shimmy down the trunk, clinging to the bark like a damn squirrel. He could have easily jumped down in one move, like I had. He saw me do it too. I kept on marching. Even when I heard him approaching through the leaves behind me. Stealthy he was not. My body flinched when he touched my shoulder from behind. Not that normal melting his touch brought.

"Wait," he requested, almost remorseful.

I didn't turn as his touch commanded. I stayed facing away, but I stopped.

"Maybe that's a little extreme. "

I crossed my arms and kept my back to him. He had a lot more to say to repair the damage he had already caused. I needed to hear him. I needed to hear my old Nathan.

"But it's necessary."

"What the hell did you just say?" I whipped around to him, and he backed up several feet once he saw my expression. "Seriously. What the hell did you just say? And please," my arms flung out and waved a fist at him. "Don't you dare say it is because Marteggo said it should."

I could tell he was trying to answer, and from the shape his lips made, I knew what the answer was.

"Let me stop you there. If Marteggo was such an outstanding role model, such a great leader, then why did he just run off when Jean challenged him? Why, over the course of several hundred years, did he never once come out of hiding? Not until I cleared the way for him. Huh? Tell me that. Tell me why you should take his rules of how to live as gospel?" I didn't wait more than half a second before I charged again. "Tell me!"

Nathan stood there with a dumbfounded expression on his face. There was no logic that supported those ridiculous and infuriating statements, at least not any I would buy.

"Let me tell you something else. I am sick and tired of hearing that name. I don't care if he is Jesus Christ of the vampires. What he told you makes no sense. We have to learn to live with others, Nathan. We have to. There is no way to truly isolate yourself and never encounter others. It's just not possible, and for those situations, you must have control. Feeding whenever you want is not that way to build up that control. You have to work at it. You... have to work at it."

Nathan looked away from me and appeared to be thinking something over. Maybe I hit a few points that made more sense than the great Marteggo. In my mind, that wasn't a hard task, but I was battling a naïve vampire that was looking up at someone with the charisma of any great cult leader.

"But..." Nathan started, still looking away from me at something off in the woods. I knew what word was going to follow that word, and I cut him off before it made it out into the open.

"What does his philosophy of life say about this?" It was a knee jerk frustration motivated reaction, and in no way in any universe, this one or any parallel one, how I planned to spring this on him, but it happened. I pulled up the sweatshirt and exposed our growing bump.

16

That wasn't even close to how I had planned to tell Nathan we were having a baby. I wanted to whisper it in his ear as we sat in my special tree, listening to the sounds of night. Then I was going to drop my little magic shield and place his hand on my stomach so he could feel and hear it. When I played that scenario out in my head, which I had countless times, I expected his reaction to be one of surprise and then joy. Of course, tons of questions would follow. I tried, an exercise in futility, to use what I had learned earlier from James to see how this would play out, but nothing came to me. I wasn't sure if it was my inability or if it was because I was trying to see my future. Of course, if I had seen how it would actually turn out, I might have changed my approach. But, like James said, that is why we can't see our own. It didn't mean I would try to cheat and see if I could.

When it finally hit Nathan what I was telling him, and it took a while, I think the shock won out over joy. He almost fell back on his ass. And probably would have if I hadn't grabbed him first. His blackened eyes stared a hole right through my belly.

"My eyes are up here," I reminded him. "Look up here." I used my hand to guide him up to my eyes. Once they were locked on to mine, I reassured him, or tried to.

"Nathan, relax, please. We are going to be fine. We are going to get through this together."

It took me a second to realize I just made this sound like some tragic disaster that we just needed to 'get' through until it was just a distant memory. I sounded frantic as I tried to correct my statements.

"It's a beautiful thing. A beautiful thing."

Jesus, if I couldn't get my thoughts and emotions together, I would never calm Nathan down any. I did what Jen taught me once and faked a deep breath. That gave me the pause my brain needed to calm down.

"What I mean is... this is wonderful and beautiful. It's nothing to be worried or afraid of. It's the start of our family."

To me, it still didn't sound any better, but it was the best I could do under the circumstances. Nathan still looked like a deer caught on a freeway full of headlights. I went with the last move I had left and dropped the little block I had up to keep Nathan from sensing its presence in me. When I did, his entire head jerked down in a split second, and his hands reached out, but stopped before they touched me.

"Go ahead." I would be lying if I said I didn't feel some apprehension about this moment, but I avoided taking any sort of defensive stance until I had a reason, and I felt I could have defended myself if he had lost control and tried to eat me. I just stood there, sweatshirt pulled up, out in the chilly night air, which surprisingly, I felt a little of against my skin. I also felt the touch of his icy fingers as they brushed across our bump before they retracted.

"It's human. I can feel the heartbeat, but how?"

Oh, lord. I knew he was going to ask that. I just hoped it wouldn't be so soon. I let my shirt down and crossed my arms over the bump. Something I had found I was doing more and more of recently. "It's kind of hard to explain, but it involves what you were before.. human.. and the other part of me... a witch."

"So, it's a witch?" He asked with a touch of vinegar.

"Slow down there. I don't know yet. Even if neither of us were vampires and were just like any human and witch having a child, there is a chance the child is born with limited or no magical abilities, like you were." I paused and let that sink in for a second, and also to see if he took that as a slight against him. It wasn't meant to be one, but even I realized it sounded that way when I said it. He didn't, or didn't show it. I think the shock of my other news had numbed him for the time being. I continued, "If they are, it takes a few years before we really know. All I know for sure is I am carrying your child, and I couldn't be happier. We are going to be a family." I realized I was now smiling from ear to ear, and not doing my normal half smile to cover my fangs, but I didn't care. He had them too. This is who we are. "Don't you want that? We talked about it once."

My boyfriend backed up, and his hand reached up and rubbed the back of his neck while he studied the situation. "Uh yeah, I just didn't expect so soon... we only.. you know... one time." And there he was. I saw it in his expression. My Nathan was back.

"Well," I said as I walked over and took his hand. "It only takes once. Didn't your mother have that talk?" I asked, in an attempt to add some levity to the situation.

"Yep, it must just be me. I'm awesome that way."

I fought the urge to push him off that pedestal of sarcasm he just stepped up on, and just appreciated the fact that was the most Nathan like thing he had said in a few days. Plus, once I tell him how this all really happened, I could remind him I am awesome in that way. That line was going into my memory tagged for use later.

"This is why you have to learn how to control things," I reminded him, bringing this all back to where we started.

"I absolutely get it now," he said without hesitation.

I wondered if he was just agreeing with me or really meant it. I hoped he did. There wasn't a clearer way to explain it to him. If he still had another opinion on the matter, it just would not work. I guess, yes, I could spend years using magic to make him see our child as a vampire, but that won't help the first time there was a paper cut or skinned knee. That I couldn't control, and what if I wasn't there? A thought that sent a shiver through me.

"You okay?" He asked, and then in a reflex of who he used to be, he put an arm around me and pulled me close.

"I'm fine." The temperature wasn't the source of my chill. Neither was the strong breeze that just blew through. It was the thought of raising our child alone if Nathan made the wrong choice. That was not a prospect I wanted to consider, but the choice really wasn't mine.

"Us, parents," he wondered aloud.

"Crazy, isn't it?" I asked, and tensed up, not knowing what his answer would be.

"Not really. I don't know about you, but I thought about it some. Just wasn't sure how it could happen. Then Amy came into our lives, and I thought maybe she was that answer. I never knew this would happen."

It was an excellent answer, and I all but exhaled. We were on the same page. Then it was his turn to tense up. He froze, and his arm fell from my shoulders.

"Crap. Amy," he whispered. "I need to get a handle on this." He looked up at me longingly. "I need to be more like you."

I turned and wrapped my arms around him. He did the same across my lower back. They were looser, not the tight embrace I am used to.

"You will," I whispered back into his ear. "I can help you. We all can. Kevin and Jen are experts at this, and Marie is the one who taught me. It just takes time." His arms tightened and his head collapsed against my shoulder.

"Thank you. I guess this life isn't as easy as others were making it sound," he bemoaned, muffled against my shoulder.

"Life is hard for everyone. Ours is just difficult in different ways than others." I cringed at how similar that sounded to something my mother said to me when I was younger.

"I guess."

"It's not a guess. It's a fact," I reassured him, and released my hold of him, backed away, and looked at his face. He was unsure about everything. This was what I expected to find once he finally woke up. I guess, just like anything else, it just took time. Having a large rowdy crowd showing him the best parts of this life and filling his head full of blissful images of what life should be like didn't really help him develop a base in reality. That would now be my job, and I had some help. But right now, I didn't want him to wallow in this. I grabbed the sides of his face and leaned in and kissed him. He kissed me back, and I felt the sparks between us, but his expression remained glum. So, I took a different path to break him out of it. I kissed him again, but before I pulled back, I said, "We're having a baby. You're going to be a daddy."

There was a spark in his eyes, and the beginning of a smile on his face. "I'm going to be a daddy. Oh god!" he gasped.

"Yes, you are. We need to celebrate this." I winked, hoping he would get my hint.

"You're right. We need to tell the others. We need to tell everyone." His face lit up, and he grabbed my hand. "Come on!" He took off running, dragging me behind him. This was not what I had in mind, but I sprinted alongside him and went along with it. Putting on a little spell while on the move to protect our bundle of joy. I wasn't ready to fight off a horde of vampires away from its beating heart.

We made our way through the shadow filled forest and continued our sprint across the fields and raced toward the house. Much to my surprise, we didn't stop there. We didn't really need to. They all knew our news, but Nathan didn't know that yet. It seemed those were the friends he intended to tell our news to. We continued straight across the field and out toward the trees where the vampires hung out. It was night, but they still sat back in the shadows and watched as we approached. Which meant they weren't staring at the witches' camp.

Nathan led us back into a clearing where the light of the full moon created a single spot surrounded by darkness. I forgot I had cleared the clouds for my little moment with Nathan. There was no point in letting the clouds return now. Nathan wanted to make an announcement, and this was the stage he chose. By all means, let's give him the spotlight.

"Marteggo! Marteggo!" he yelled. I thought he wanted to tell everyone, but it seemed he only wanted to tell one person. His summonsing attracted many others in the woods to come forth and step to the edge of the light. Among them I spied Mike and Clay. It wasn't long before Marteggo emerged from behind them with Theodora wrapped around his arm. The crowd parted as he stepped through and into the center.

"Master Saxon, good evening."

"We have great news," started Nathan. He looked down at me, bursting at the seams. I looked at Theodora, who looked like the cat who ate the canary. "We are going to have a baby. Larissa is pregnant."

Marteggo looked at him curiously, then bellowed a hearty laugh. "Me thinks young Nathan here drank blood from a local drunk." The assembled mass of vampires laughed. That was all except three. Theodora, Mike, and Clay knew the truth.

"It's true, I tell you," insisted Nathan. "She let me feel its pulse. It's there." He hastily reached for my shirt, and I slapped his hand away. I wasn't ready for him to yank my shirt up in front of this large of a crowd.

Marteggo laughed again and released Theodora before circling around the spot of moonlight, taking center stage. "It's all right Nathan. We've all had it happen before. Those that walk Bourbon Street are easy marks, and depending on what they drank, they can be really sweet." He walked up and threw an arm around Nathan. "Now come. Let's go tell more stories and find a feast."

Nathan shook the man's arm off, and there was a collective murmur among the gathering. Everyone stepped back, and Marteggo turned and regarded Nathan sternly. This was bad. Nathan had disrespected Marteggo. He didn't mean to, and I knew that, but that was how it looked to everyone else. I tried to take a step in between the two men, but Nathan forced me back behind him.

Clay and Mike had left the group and moved forward. I had seen that look in Mike's eyes before. Things were escalating, and you could feel the egos of each man approaching their boiling points.

"It is true," said Theodora. Dozens of heads spun around and looked at her. Marteggo was the last. She stood there in the moonlight, almost leery of the collective gazes. "It is true. How we don't know, but Larissa is carrying Nathan's child. I was there when she found out. I felt the child's presence myself."

"You're sure?" Marteggo asked her gruffly.

She nodded and shrank as he walked toward her.

"So, it's true?" he asked, towering over her.

"Yes," she replied as his large hand reached under her chin and tilted her head up forcing her to look into his eyes. She shied away from his gaze when she answered. He held her there for a few moments, waiting for their eyes to lock, but they never did. The love I saw between them before was all but gone. Her head shook in his grasp, and I realized there was a different dynamic between them. It was the first time I had seen it. Then I realized it wasn't just between them, it was with everyone. There was an electric tension in the air, so thick you could cut it with a blunt knife. When Marteggo finally let go of his beloved's chin, it ratcheted down, but just slightly to an uneasiness. Everyone waited for his reaction as he backed away from Theodora slowly. There was a low growl that evolved into a quiet but deep chuckle. It increased in volume and intensity as he turned around with a wide grin.

"Then we must celebrate," he announced and threw his arms out. The gathered masses cheered and rushed in to offer their congratulations.

Mike made his way through the crowd and hugged me like so many others had. He held on longer than the others. He pulled me closer and whispered, "What the hell was that?"

"No clue," I replied. I didn't really have one, but I was just as curious as Mike was, if not more so.

When he backed away, he looked at me and at Marteggo. I had seen that face before. It was the same look Mike had regarded Clay with the night we first met him up on the roof. Marteggo had lost Mike's trust.

I kept a close watch on Marteggo as I endured the parade of hugs. He kept one eye on me the whole time and kept his distance.

I spent hours hearing prospective baby names from all the women. Some had had children before they became vampires. Others were extremely jealous, never having the chance themselves. A few were uncomfortably jealous. Not really making eye contact when they talked. Just kind of looking to my side and being polite as their friends gushed. I had a feeling they came along to avoid being the one or two that hung in the darkness during what appeared to be such a joyous occasion. I understood. The jealousy, not the coming along with their friends. Well, maybe I understood both. I wasn't exactly that excited to be here. Being mobbed was not exactly my cup of tea, but I was here because of Nathan.

Once the mob cleared, the night turned into rounds of singing and dancing. I conveniently used my condition as an excuse to avoid both. Everyone bought it, but it also backfired. Throughout the night I was once again mobbed, well not really mobbed more like had my peace interrupted by the rather frequent visit of someone asking if I felt okay and comfortable. Each time, I said I was, which I was, except I was being bothered. I just wanted to sit there and watch.

I could see why Kevin had said Nathan was coming along well. He was in the middle of it all, with no hesitation. The social butterfly, as it were, with his girlfriend, the wallflower sitting over here on a stump. It was good to see, mostly. Seeing how he followed Marteggo around like a lost puppy made my skin crawl. He wasn't the only one. Men and women alike hung on every word of his stories, and boy did he have stories. I never once saw that man not in the center of a large group with his mouth flapping.

"Doing all right?"

I looked up at Clay. "If another damn person asks me that, they might get punched."

"Yep, you're fine," he remarked and sat down next to me.

"What? Are you tired of the Marteggo show?"

"I'm not much for large groups of people, plus…" Clay stopped.

"Plus, what?"

"I don't know. Maybe it's just me, but there is something about him I don't like. Something about all his stories. They are just too over the top."

"Doth he exaggerate?" I asked, going a little over the top with my old English myself.

"1000%. If he is what he says he is, how did Jean ever push him out?"

"Exactly!" I exclaimed, causing a few to look in our direction. I just waved in return and turned my head toward Clay. "Sorry, but that is exactly the same question I have."

"I know he said it was something about Jean getting the masses behind him, but I bet Marteggo could have yanked that string bean of a man's head off before he even knew he was there. All you have to do is look through history and you know the masses follow whoever holds the power. The masses would have followed him, again."

"Why Clayton Lindsey, what an astute observation." I all but fanned myself. I had to admit my southern drawl was getting better.

"Hey, world history was my favorite class back in school," he smiled back, but that smile was short-lived. He slumped next to me. "Man, that was just a few months ago, but it feels like a lifetime away."

"I know Clay." I draped my arm around him and gave him a comforting squeeze. "I know. Just being here brings back so many memories, but they don't feel like mine anymore. It's like I am looking…"

"At someone else's life?" he asked.

"Exactly."

"It's strange," remarked Clay. "Speaking of strange." His head jerked to the right and mine followed. He was right, here comes strange. Marteggo was coming in our direction.

"I should give you guys some privacy," suggested Clay. He stood up.

I grabbed onto his hand and yanked him hard back down toward the stump. "Don't you dare."

"You'll be fine, and I won't be far." He yanked free and meandered away, and he was right. He wasn't far away. He found a comfortable tree just a few yards away, but far enough to not look like he was lingering or hovering. His eyes watched Marteggo with a suspicious gaze. Marteggo didn't appear to notice that Clay, or that anyone else was even there. It was just me and him.

Marteggo stopped right in front of me and waited. Was I to stand, or stay seated in his presence? I didn't know. So, I stayed seated, and watched his reaction. There was no mistaking it. He was studying me, and I didn't like it. His magical charisma may have wooed Nathan. It had no effect on me. I saw a man who was a walking irony.

"I want to give you my congratulations," he said and clicked on the charm.

"You already did. Don't you remember? Right after Nathan told everyone, you came up and gave me a hug," I replied flatly. I wanted to see how he would respond to someone correcting him, and it appeared I was the only one that had the guts to try. Everyone else hung onto every word that parted his lips, like it was the gospel.

He didn't seem to like it at first, and hesitated before he responded. Was he trying to remember back to see if he had or was there another thought going through his head? Maybe trying to think of a response. Maybe thinking of how to dispose of me quickly. "I did, didn't I," he said, and again attempted to turn on the charm, and then sat next to me on my stump. He didn't even ask.

"I must say, I am still confused how it happened. I have met several humans carrying the child of a vampire, but never two vampires. Perhaps it has something to do with you being a witch."

I had to give it to him. He was smarter and sharper than I expected. He made that leap faster than anyone else.

"It's a possibility we have to consider. My being a witch brings many things into play." To give him a little of a reminder, I held open a hand in front of him and let a small flame dance across the surface. The sight mesmerized him. Like so many, he fell victim to the shiny object phenomenon. Show them something they haven't seen, or don't see often, and you will have them eating out of the palm of your hand, at least until the next shiny object appeared.

"Speaking of. I hear you are still undergoing training with the outcasts." He pointed out of the trees and in the direction of the orange flickering glow of the witches' camp.

"I am. Several of the rogue witches," the second time I corrected him in a very short time, and I still had my head, "are helping to provide me with refreshers. I spent so long away from the world of magic after Jean's followers turned me. I have forgotten a few things."

"That's good," he started, and then shifted and turned toward me. "But don't forget, you are a vampire. You really should spend time out here with Nathan and the rest of us learning about us. If I remember correctly, you were raised in isolation by the Nortons. I'm sure they did the best they could, but that is no way to raise a vampire."

Did he really just insult the Nortons and me? Could he really be that full of himself? It was time to knock him down a rung or two, respectfully, or as respectfully as I could. "If you are talking about knowing what we are, knowing how to hunt, and knowing how to control things so we can be part of the world, we did just fine. I have been around others for a while now with no issue and can go weeks in between feedings without losing control." I tamped down how offended I felt by his assertion, and tried to the best of my ability to not sound overly proud or boasting, but I was afraid that slipped out at the end.

"Several weeks?" He asked, almost scoffing. "Impressive. But what I speak of is not about knowing how to control yourself. It's about knowing who and what you are, and suckling up to the world to repay you for this curse it gave you."

"I'll pass. I like the way I'm living my life."

"As a witch," he added to my statement.

"As both a witch and a vampire," I corrected.

Marteggo groaned and placed both of his huge hands on his knees and pushed up off of my stump and stood up and stretched. "That was what I meant."

I was sure it wasn't, and he was trying to save face. I wasn't keeping score, but this was the third time I had corrected him in the last several minutes.

"Tell me? Is Marcus Meridian one of the witches instructing you in that camp?" he asked, without turning to face me.

"He is one of many," I replied shortly.

"Huh," he grunted, and then walked back to the crowd in the middle of the clearing

17

I wasn't sure how long the impromptu party went on, but I left well before dawn. I pleaded for Nathan to come back with me, but he resisted, wanting to stay for a while longer. I tried to explain that I couldn't. Before I went out for my daily training, I wanted to take a shower and spend some time with Amy. That brought on another round of his tantrum about how much time I spent with the witches and ignoring my other side. My little sarcastic wave of my hand around at all the vampires I had spent all night with didn't seem to make the point I wanted. Nathan used to understand how important all this was, but the great and wonderful Marteggo had clouded his vision. Mike and Clay promised me they would look after him, but I got a feeling they were going to watch more than that.

By the time I had showered and changed, the more traditional way because it just felt more normal, the rest of the house buzzed with activity. There was the normal jockeying for the one and only bathroom. A detail I hadn't considered as much of a problem before. At least not until Mrs. Saxon sent the others here. Now it was a problem. But it was a problem that could be easily fixed from the comfort of my room with a little magical renovation. I hadn't learned how to make my own magical space like the coven or my father's office yet, so I stole the coat closet in the hall and made it into a small bathroom with a standup shower in it. It was cramped, but effective. Steve was the first to discover the renovation, and yelled down the stairs, "Hey guys, did you know we have two bathrooms?"

Once the stampede up the stairs finished, I left my bedroom, silently. I think Martin and Cynthia noticed me as I walked by. It was the first time, other than when she was around Amy, that I had seen that girl do so much as crack a smile. I went downstairs and started fixing breakfast. Now that was a first, or make that a first in the last eighty years. The smell didn't bother me as much as it had before, and I even snuck a strip of bacon. To say that everyone was surprised when they entered the kitchen and saw me standing over a table with all the fixings.. well, they were. But I didn't care about everyone. I cared about that smile Amy had on her face. She was 'the *why*' to why I did all this. It had nothing to do with that nagging voice in my head that complained over and over about my neglecting her. Okay, maybe it did.

I sat across the table from her and drew a smiley face with butter in her grits. Then I used a piece of bacon to make a smile on another plate with two eggs as the eyes. That produced the third smile, the one I wanted to see most of all. The one on that girl's face.

When I stole the strip of bacon off her plate, she attempted to snatch it back from me, but she was a little too slow for me. I wasn't really trying. Maybe I should have been, though. Amy fell back laughing in her chair when the bacon left my hand and floated back onto her plate. I looked down at the end of the table at both Jack and Lisa. Neither was owning up to being the one that robbed me of one more taste of that salty paradise.

Luckily for them, I forgave both of them quickly. Lisa had told Jack of our little adventure the day before, and now he wanted to come along. Which wasn't really a problem. Jack had been out to the witches' camp several times, but hey if he wanted to come along today for our new version of witch's school, then class was in session.

Amy came along as well. I tried to tell her no. Today wasn't going to be as much fun, even though only portions of it were fun yesterday. It was mostly frustrating. James appeared to be the only one enjoying our little session, while Lisa and I struggled to master the skill. I can't even consider it that. We were so far from any form of mastery of this skill, it wasn't even funny. We were barely beginners, and I had already failed to follow through with my promise to practice on my own last night. I doubt James would accept my excuse of being a little busy. Of course, if he was the master he appeared to be, he would already know it was coming.

Lisa spent the entire walk into camp bragging about all the homework she had done last night. She even had Jack wondering if he could perform the same feat. Lisa didn't hesitate to throw a wet blanket over his hopes, reminding him how rare of a skill it was.

Where we were going today was a far rarer skill, and I would be lying if I said I didn't feel a few butterflies about it. It wasn't the morning sickness, or whatever it was called either. I hadn't gotten sick in about a day in a half, which on this accelerated schedule, I guess, was more like a few weeks. Maybe it was the bacon I had consumed. That was a possibility, but the most likely source was all the warnings Edward had given me about this very topic. The stack of books he produced on the same topic still sat next to the bed in my room in the coven.

As we entered the witches' camp, I noticed something odd off in the distance. There were always vampires lingering just inside the shadows of the tree line. Some watched the witches, and others didn't. They were just there. Today was a little different, though. The crowd was larger, and there was no denying it. They were all watching the witches' camp. Especially one particular vampire. Marteggo was at the front of the line. He appeared interested, watching us as we walked from the house to the camp.

"So, we aren't seeing James today?" Lisa asked, annoyed. Her head twisted around and looked at his tent as we passed by.

"Nope, but if you had been practicing, you would have already known that."

She ignored my little jab. I believe there was something more personal that had her distracted. The deep sigh behind me confirmed that. Now I was the one that should have seen that coming. He was rather easy on the eyes, and rather, well, electric to be around. I'd be lying if I didn't feel the charge.

"Today, we are going to see Mary Smith. She's a rather pleasant person." I said with a straight face. The one and only time I ever met Mary, she didn't appear to be a fan of mine. It wouldn't be farfetched to say she would rather burn me at the stake than hug me. "Her specialty is descensum."

The rhythmic footsteps that had followed me all the way from the house vanished. I only heard Amy's and mine. There were also two rather panicked thumpings behind me. I turned and saw two very slack jaw witches staring back at me. "You guys coming?"

"Larissa, you do know what that is?" whispered Lisa.

I nodded. "Yep. Astral project, and trust me, I know how dangerous this is. Edward told me all about it once."

"Nooooo." Lisa shook her head back and forth violently, and she wasn't whispering now. She reached over and grabbed my arm and pulled me toward her. "Think about the word. Descensum."

Lisa stared deeply into my eyes. Searching for understanding, which I had to admit, I didn't have a bloody clue what she was getting at.

"Descend?" she asked, with a hand pointing down.

I stared back, "And?"

"Larissa, she means down under," interjected Jack nervously. "The afterlife. The underworld. The nether. The place where souls go when you die."

"Oh. OH!" The term finally hit me. I was to descend to the world of the afterlife and come back. That was a detail Marcus Meridian and Master Thomas had left out, and probably for good reason. That sounded all sorts of Halloween ghost story and horror film creepy. The more I thought about it, the more the second thoughts grew about taking any visits to the world of the dead. Even if it was just a short one. Then a thought occurred to me and all but swept those away. "I've already done it," I whispered to myself. "I've already done it," I said louder and looked at Lisa. Then I said it again while looking at Jack. "My visits to my mother. Don't you see? I've already done it. I've done it dozens of times."

"No. No, you haven't. Not this," Lisa explained. Panic dripped from her voice. "That is a family connection. It's different. I had an aunt that did this to connect people with lost loved ones. Larissa," she grabbed both of my heads, and lowered her head. "After she did it, she wasn't right for several days, and even then, she was different. It took something out of her, and she refused to talk about what it was like. She only told the family what their relative said, nothing more."

Well, if the prospect didn't sound exciting before, it definitely didn't now. I only had to do it once for the test. Well, maybe twice. Once in practice to know I could do it, and then once in the test of the seven wonders, or whatever that thing was called. Too bad it wasn't multiple choice, and I couldn't just identify what the wonders were. This was a damn essay test from hell, with one paragraph dedicated to a visit to either heaven or hell. Then that had me wondering. Which would I visit? Which brought another question. Were there really two different places? Holy spinning confusion, Batman. I was now pondering the existence of life after death. A topic discussed and argued in so many forums, from art to religion. If I did this right, I might have some answers. I wasn't sure I really wanted those answers.

"Maybe someone should take Amy back to the house," I strongly suggested.

Amy rejected the notion just as strongly by wrapping herself around my leg with a death grip. I felt each of her fingers pressing through my jeans. Luckily, I didn't bruise. Neither Jack nor Lisa volunteered to help there.

"Well…" I stuttered as I tried to think of an excuse not to continue forward. There were a few. Maybe more than a few, but they were all selfish and temporary. I had to remember that this was just a step on the only path that will solve the problems that stood between me and any chance of a peaceful life. I had given up on the notion of a normal life. This step was just a very unpleasant sounding one, but there was no avoiding it. As I saw it, it was a trade-off. A little temporary terror now to avoid long-term hell in the future. Not that looking at it that way made it any less frightening of a proposition. I just had to do it. "Let's go."

We walked right up to Mary Smith's tent. There was no one outside waiting for us. There wasn't really anything outside except a string of what appeared to be a wash. I wasn't sure if we should walk right in or not. Our last encounter wasn't exactly welcoming. The problem with tents? There are no doors to knock on. I guess I could knock on the flap that blocked the opening, but I doubt that would make any noise at all. Lisa gave me a slight poke from behind as I stood there, trying to decide how to proceed. I hate to tell her. If she pokes me again, I was going to throw her through the flap, solving our problem.

I settled on what I thought was the only acceptable option. "Mary Smith, are you home?"

"Yes. Yes," her scratchy voice responded from behind the flap. "Come on in, I guess."

So far, the same warmth as before. I tried to imagine what I might find beyond the flap. A large estate like Marcus's tent? Perhaps an apartment like what I saw when we visited James. Both appeared to be too stylish for this woman, but one never knows. Appearances can deceive, though I had my doubts. I stepped in wondering about a third option, but arrived in one that never crossed my mind, and it probably wouldn't have. I moved in further and let the others join me in the small tent. It was just that, a tent. The same patchwork tent we saw from the outside. Candles and lanterns were everywhere, casting a host of flickering shadows of the tent posts and furniture against the fabric walls.

"You brought others," she said with a hint of disdain. Mary walked in, wearing a black dress and a shawl over her shoulders. A large green pendant hung from her neck, and small glasses struggled to hang on to the end of her nose as she studied the others.

"No vampires. These two are witches, and this one," I placed my hand on top of Amy's hand, "she is a shapeshifter."

"I know that. I'm not stupid, you know. Do they know what you are here for?" she asked suspiciously.

"Yes."

"And they know what this really is?" she asked, and then pointed a gnarled finger at Lisa and said, "I imagine you do. The darkness is within you, but you have firm control of it. Good. Good." She almost sounded pleased when she turned her attention to Jack. "You, on the other hand, are just a witch." Mary turned her back and walked around the center post in the tent.

I looked back at Lisa who struggled to hold in the grin at that little slap. I put that one away to use later and hid any joy I felt about the grimace on Jack's face.

"Well, come on. If we're going to do this, we need to do this right." Mary motioned for us to follow her. Where were we going? I wasn't sure. There wasn't much room in the tent, but then I realized. She wasn't here when we first walked in. She came from somewhere. So, we followed her around the center post, and toward a dark void that appeared in the side wall of the tent.

If we were some place different, I wasn't sure. It was possible we were still in the tent, just another part of it that was on the back of it. This wasn't a large space, and there were no windows or anything to give a sense of where we might be. It was dark, except for a single candle in the middle of a symbol I recognized quite well. We all did, but for different reasons. It was a pentagram.

"Each of you sit at one of the points. I will sit here," she said, her voice gravelly and wandering. "Sit quickly."

Lisa and Jack both picked a point. I maneuvered Amy to the two open ones, making sure she sat between me and either Lisa or Jack. Since we entered, or make that since Mary entered, Amy had clung to my side. Something about her presence, and maybe her appearance, made Amy leery. I completely understood. This whole thing made me leery.

"You probably all know what this is, and I am sure you think you understand its significance, but you are probably wrong, so I will tell you to make sure you don't do anything stupid. This is a pentagram. The perfect shape. It is made up of ten interlocking triangles. Each triangle is the perfect ratio. That perfection solidifies the strength and the protection the symbol provides us." Her hand traced over the shape drawn in white. Each line shimmered as her hand passed over it. "This symbol is not the source of any darkness. It is protection against the darkness, and it will protect those of us that travel to the other side and help guide us back." She leaned forward and leered at the three of us. "Now leave any stupid misconceptions you have about this symbol, and accept what I have told you. You have to do that or leave."

She paused as if she were waiting for someone to walk out. None of us moved other than to look at one another.

"Okay, then. Let's begin. First, you need one of these." Mary waved her hand over the candle in the center. A haze surrounded it, and when it disappeared, a wide black candle appeared. The flame that was there before lost its yellow hue. It itself was black and danced around. A fine line of black smoke rose from it and circled around the room overhead. It was strange looking. Unbroken, like a string, or a thin thread.

"This is a reunion candle. Its smoke is the guide for your astral self. It rises and weaves like a single unbroken string. Focus on it. Follow it. There is nothing in this world but it. It will lead you to the afterlife and back. It's up to you to follow it. To become one with it, but, and you must not forget this, don't let go of it. If you do, you will be lost and will never return."

Mary paused after the warning, and I watched the smoke rise and circle around the room. It was beautiful and creepy all at once. It danced like one of those cobras in a basket. Its movements were slow and fluid, almost poetic.

"Watch the smoke. Grab hold of the smoke. When you feel it pulling you, don't resist. Go with it. Just don't let go."

It happened almost instantly as the smoke circled around me. I was moving, but my body wasn't. It was a weird sensation, to say the least. I was floating, but I still felt like I was sitting firmly on the floor. When the smoke passed by, I reached out and grabbed it. My physical hand never moved, but I had a firm hold on the smoke and as it continued by, I followed it.

"You feel it, Larissa? Don't you?" Mary asked. Her voice had lost the disdain and scratchiness it had when we first arrived. Now it was clear and smooth. Almost rhythmic.

"I do," I replied, but my voice said nothing. It was just a thought.

"Good," Mary said, or thought. She was there with me, wherever I was, just like Mrs. Tenderschott was when I used those potions. "Now yank the string. Yank it hard."

I looked down at the string. I had a firm hold of it, but didn't feel it. Even though it had wrapped itself around my hand and up my arm.

"Larissa! Yank it! Now!"

I gave it a firm yank, and I found myself again sitting on the floor at the point of the pentagram. Behind me, Amy lay asleep with her head in Jack's lap. He was almost asleep, too. Mary was not on her point. She was sitting right next to me, looking at me. Her expression and body language were not one I had seen from her before.

"Congratulations Larissa. You just did your first free float." Her hand reached out and touched my shoulder. "How do you feel?"

"Okay?" I said, but it was really more of a question. I didn't have a clue what she was talking about, or how I was supposed to feel after I did whatever it was she said I did. "Was that it?"

"No," she said. Then Mary looked at Lisa. "Welcome back Lisa." Mary blew out the black candle, and it changed back to the tall white one. She removed it from the center of the pentagram and then took its place, sitting in front of me and Lisa. "That was not it. That was just the first step. Unfortunately, Jack doesn't have the gift." She looked through the gap between the two of us and back at Jack to address him. "Don't take it hard. All witches are different. They all have different talents. Some are better at some types of magic than others." She pointed at Lisa, but smiled when she did. "Lisa comes from the dark side of magic. This is more natural to her." Then she turned to me. "You don't, but you have the talent. This was just your first step out of your body. Simple astral projection. You didn't go far. That was because I wouldn't let you. At least not yet. I had control of the smoke. I needed to see who could, and how easily they could. Now that I know, we can take a few further treks, and then make the one you seek. If that is what you want."

She stood up out of the center and extended her hands to both of us, helping us up to our feet. "You need your rest now before we make any further attempts." She looked directly at me with a smirk. "She needs her rest. You don't, but you should wait a little longer before trying again."

"Thank you, I said, trying to forget the woman I first met, and take in the one that was here now. I liked this one better. I gathered Amy off of Jack's lap. She was still sleepy, so I picked her up and carried her. It was no problem. Jack yawned when he stood up. We followed Mary back into her main tent and to the door. When we stepped out, night had fallen, the moon was high in the sky, and campfires illuminated the camp. I turned around, surprised.

"How long were we here?"

"Too long," Jack said between yawns.

"About ten hours," replied Mary Smith. "It didn't seem like more than a few minutes, did it?"

I shook my head. It didn't. It didn't feel like more than a minute or two.

"That's the danger of projection. You can lose track of time, place, and your own existence if you go too deep. While you were under and taking the first steps to separate your consciousness from your body, Amy and Jack and I had several nice conversations and we even had lunch."

There was that feeling that I had a little too much over the last several months. The spinning head of confusion. Ten hours in just a few moments? Wow! Losing track of time was right. I felt completely lost as it was. One of Edward's warnings played in my head. It was about getting lost, and not doing it for more than an hour. What was it I read about that? Oh yea, the fact that the world would have moved too far for you to find your way back to your physical vessel. But wait! I had been out for ten hours and still managed.

"Larissa, are you all right? You look pale, even for a vampire."

I looked right at Mary and asked, "How was that possible? Ten hours. I have heard... I mean, read that if we are away from ourselves for anything around an hour or longer, we can't find our way back."

Mary lit up. "You have studied this before. That's great."

"Just some reading. I don't understand how..."

"The smoke," interrupted Mary. "The smoke created a construct you could hang on to find your way back. When I told you to yank it, that pulled you back. Remember, I told you to never let go of it. If you had, you could have been lost."

18

Amy slept in my arms all the way back up to the house. I wanted to wake her when we got there to make sure she ate, but she was so soundly asleep, I hated to wake her. I took her up to her own room and laid her down. I'd make sure she ate when she woke up. There were no set meal times in this house. Except for Rob and Martin. They explained they had to eat every four hours to keep up their awesomeness, and man did they eat. They mowed down a table full of food quickly, but yet there wasn't a pound of fat on their frames. Now that we weren't at the coven, they ran around in not much more than a pair of shorts and shoes. Being what they were, I wondered why they even bothered with the shoes.

I closed the door carefully after taking one last peek at Amy. She looked so peaceful, and I had to admit, I was a bit envious. To have just one moment like that would be wonderful. I made my way to the stairs and found someone waiting for me at the bottom. And knew this would not be one of those moments.

"You didn't have to leave," said Nathan.

He didn't look pleased. Talk about holding something in. It had been well over twelve hours since I left that little party. I held a finger up to my lips, but he missed the message.

"Why? What was so important?" he demanded.

I grabbed his arm when I was on the bottom step and yanked him into the parlor. "Amy's asleep," I said and closed the double glass doors behind us. "Keep it down, please."

At that, Nathan looked a little sheepish, but that didn't deter his inquisition. "You left our party. Everyone was celebrating something that never happens, and you just disappeared." He marched toward me, and I was having nothing of his little display, and met him halfway with a hand on his chest.

"First!," I emphasized to make the first of many points I had. "I never asked for that party. I just wanted to tell you. Most everyone that mattered already knew. THEY were awake when I was sick and had the first signs." I should have thought about that point a little more before I made it. I only meant to say I didn't ask for a party. The rest of it just kind of came out, but it took some of the air out of his sails. "Second," I said, this time with a little less punch, "I told you I was leaving. I had an appointment."

"I know. More witch shit," he snapped.

"Yes, more witch stuff," I corrected him, and then turned to put some space between us in the hopes it might lower the tension in the room. "Remember, I am part witch, and I also shouldn't have to remind you about everything that is going on. Remember Jean St. Claire? The one who turned you into this? Mrs. Wintercrest, who isn't really my biggest fan, and now an ally of Jean St. Claire? Then there is the problem Master Thomas and Mr. Demius have asked for my help with? All of these... every one of them, is something standing in the way of our long and happy life and requires me to learn and master more magic. So, yes, more witch stuff. It is a mandatory part of life."

He paced back and forth, stewing. I wondered if I had gone too far with my first point, but it was how things happened, and eventually someone was bound to slip up and say something. It was better he heard it from me.

"Do I need to remind you? You are a vampire, too?"

"You don't, and if you think you need to, then you are stupid." There was no regret in using that word. Everything reminded me I was a vampire. Everything. "There isn't a moment that goes by that doesn't remind me. I have been one for eighty years, you have been one for a couple of days. Don't you dare lecture me." My finger wagged at him, and I had to resist the urge to let something else enter this discussion. Sending him against the wall wouldn't accomplish anything.

"Then why not focus on that for a bit? Spend more time with me out there with them. Help me get to know them, and myself."

Nathan's eyes begged, and I felt a little of my frustration melt. There was an olive branch I could offer that I hoped would end this. "If I promise to spend more time out there with you, will you understand why I need to spend the time I do with the witches? This is bigger than you and I, but it directly impacts what kind of life *we* will have." I did something I had only seen in movies and rubbed that bump of a belly I had to remind him that the *we* I referred to was more than just he and I.

"I think I can accept that," he agreed reluctantly.

I dropped my guard and walked over to him with every intention of making up the best way I could. Only to be stopped by the utter stupidity of his next comment.

"If you would consider a future without magic. We could live away from everyone and not have to worry about anything."

"Wait right there!" I stepped back for his own benefit. "We already discussed this."

"No!" he interrupted. "We didn't. We talked about my need to learn control because of our child, and I agreed. We never discussed not living secluded from others, for our safety and theirs. Marteggo's lifestyle has some benefits."

"I never want to hear that name again!" I turned away and squeezed my hands at the end of my very straight arms.

"Why? He has valid points."

"Seriously?" I asked with my back still to him. Points were running through my head, and some were rather childish and hurtful. Not really beneath me at the moment, but again, it wouldn't accomplish anything, and I needed to end this discussion with Nathan agreeing with me. That was the only acceptable outcome. But what if he didn't? What if he never bent on that? What then? That was a question that had only one answer, and it was one I didn't want to face at the moment.

I turned around, doing my best to appear loving and understanding, but God help Nathan if he mentioned that man's name one more time. Actually, I was going to commit that sin, but only once, and I hoped that would be the end of it. Hopes rarely reflect reality and his proximity out there, and the constant visits the others made told me that the name was going to be a fixture for the time being. Maybe I could diminish how it was used.

"Nathan, Marteggo didn't live that lifestyle until Jean forced him to leave! Before, he lived in the city and enjoyed everything that early New Orleans offered. So don't fall for what he is selling. He settled. But let me remind you of something I shouldn't have to. The Nortons tried that, and they still found us. It doesn't work. If it did, I would have never come to the coven. We would have never met, and this moment would never happen." Now, let's see Mr. Dreamboat comeback at that with any pearls of wisdom from the great and powerful Marteggo.

He pondered that for a few seconds. I saw the wheels churning in his head. Which caused mine to turn and anticipate whatever counter argument he was evaluating before he said it aloud. I hoped he was carefully considering everything. If he was, then he would realize there was nothing he could say. I was the living example of that theoretical life. An experiment gone very wrong, with the same variables at play. Someone was trying to find us while we were hiding. Mr. Markinson would be so proud that I remembered the scientific method, though I doubt he would have ever thought this would be how I applied it.

"True," he reluctantly conceded, and I felt the weight of the world leave. That left the other half-a-dozen worlds I was still involved with pressing on me, but at least one was gone. I inched forward, feeling victorious. "But can't you leave magic behind and just be one of us?"

And to think I was about to reward him with a kiss. "Why? Please, oh please tell me why? What and whose great wisdom has led to request that?" If I heard that name, forget restraint. Nathan was going into the wall behind him. Maybe it would knock some sense into him. I was ready for it, and I practically dared him to say it.

"Questions are the search for reason. It was just a request. A lot of our problems come from you being a witch." He paused, and then I watched his lips form that name, but he stopped before he said it. "I believe life would be easier if you just picked one."

"If only it were that easy." I saw the look on his face and knew I had just walked into something. Something I should have seen it coming from a mile away before I threw that softball at him. I had to stop it before he took the opening. "Uh. Uh. Uh. Before you say it is. Think about it like this. Biologically, I am a vampire. I can't do anything about that, no matter how much I wanted to choose otherwise. Magic flows around and through me. It's like breathing to a human. I can't ignore it. It's in everything we do. You should understand that. Your mother is a witch."

"But you could just ignore it. It can still flow," he flailed his arms in the air, "around you, but you just ignore it. Isn't that what you do when you blend in?" Nathan put air quotes around the words blend-in, and I knew what he was trying to say, but I was about to drop a bomb-shell on him that might think otherwise and remove any of that brainwashing hogwash the last few nights surrounded by vampires might have infused into him.

"Remember, vampires stop acting like vampires to blend in, too. Jen and Kevin teach an entire class about that. It goes both ways, with one exception. Magic is wonderful. Why would I want to ignore that?" I shouldn't, and nothing he or anyone could say would convince me otherwise. It felt it was the side that gave me life, and I couldn't even believe he was trying to talk me into leaving it behind. Why? To become something that lives in the darkness? One of the world's despised and feared creatures? But I had one more card to play, and it was, I hoped, a mic drop moment. "Plus, magic is why we have this." My hand patted my stomach.

Stunned wasn't the right word for his appearance. Shocked? Knocked for a loop? About to pass out? Those might be better, but still seemed to fall short. He stood there, visibly shaken, looking right at what I had directed his attention to.

"Why would I want to ignore magic?"

"You..." he started and then looked up at me. Words escaped him as he attempted to construct a sentence that anyone who spoke English would understand. "... created that?"

I guess I needed to explain and wondered if I needed to go into the biologics involved with being a vampire, but I didn't want it to sound like a science class. "Kind of," I started while I searched for how. Whatever he had that robbed him of the English language seemed to be contagious. The basics. Just the basics. I reminded myself. "When you become a vampire, your body stops changing. So, a female vampire's body can't change to carry a child."

"So, you created one!" he exclaimed, pointing violently at our child.

"No," I urged him to slow down and let me finish. "I didn't. Not in the way you mean. It is ours. When we were having sex, I let a thought slip through, and the magic took over."

I felt that should have explained it well enough for him to understand that it was ours, but it only existed because of magic. Hopefully, he wouldn't look at magic as something we could just ignore or want to live without, no matter who was filling his skull of mush with anything different. Hopefully, he would look at something other than my stomach. I was about to remind him where my eyes were when I saw his face turn grim.

"That's an aberration," he screamed. Then Nathan's body crashed into the far wall, pulverizing the plaster behind him. I let both of my hands hang out away from my body, glowing, to remind him to choose his next words carefully.

Rob and Jack rushed in through the double doors. "What the hell?"

They stopped and looked at Nathan, who was nothing but a groaning pile of humanity under a plaster dust cloud.

"Ask him." I pointed right at Nathan to make sure they knew the *him* I was referring to. "He seems to think our baby is an aberration. That's the word you used, right?"

"Larissa, put it away." Jack held up a hand defensively in my direction and I dropped my hands, and with them, the bright glowing orbs they held.

Now others had joined the crowd at the door. Mike, Laura, and Apryl were the first to come. Brad and Clay were next.

"Sure everyone, come on in. It's just a private conversation. That is why the doors were closed." I motioned toward the doors that Rob and Jack had opened.

"Well, you're the one who about brought the house down," remarked Apryl. Mike and Brad helped Nathan up to his feet. He kept his distance, and he was smart to do so. I loved him, but he had a lot of thinking to do and needed to start saying the right things.

"That child she is carrying. It's magic. It's not real."

Every head in the room swung around first in my direction, but when I held up two empty hands, they turned back to Nathan with shocked expressions.

"Nathan, it's a real child. Flesh and blood. We have all felt it." Apryl turned to me. "Did you let him feel it?"

I nodded.

Apryl turned back to him. "Then you felt it too. What the hell are you talking about? Yes, maybe magic that let her conceive and carry the child, but that doesn't mean it isn't real, and it is yours. You two made that baby. Just like anyone else." She lectured him harshly, and he didn't seem to appreciate it. He looked at her at first, but then avoided eye contact and squirmed where he stood.

By now others had joined the party, and Jennifer Bolden had taken up position behind Apryl. She had obviously heard what our little disagreement was about and appeared none too happy. When Apryl gave her an open, she pounced like a protective mother would.

"Look Nathan. No matter how that child came to be. You and Larissa are having a miracle. You should both be happy. Now get whatever stupid thoughts you have out of your head, and man up. Your mother would have expected better from you. You and I both know that."

Jen meant well and had a room full of nodding heads. But one head didn't follow suit. She lit a fuse inside that one that went off violently. "My mother would have sided with the witches because she was one. There is a better life out there without magic. You all are just too blinded by the lies of the witches to see it." He pushed free of Mike and Clay and knocked Apryl and Jen down on their way. Mike took offense to that and went to grab Nathan. Nathan tossed him aside with little effort. Clay thought he had him, but Nathan swung around and grabbed him by the throat. His throat strained under Nathan's grip. There was nothing stopping him from popping Clay's head off just by squeezing, like the top off a tube of toothpaste.

A chorus of voices called for him to stop, and I screamed at him to let Clay go. I was ready to strike when Rob hit Nathan with a tackle in the ribs that loosened both his grip and more plaster from the wall. Clay slipped to the floor and retreated. His hands explored his neck for proof that his head was still attached. Apryl ran to him. It was a good thing too. She restrained Clay and kept him from following Nathan as he fled out the door and out of the house. We all knew where he was heading, and to me that felt more devastating than what had just happened, and that had me collapsing down on the settee with my head in my hands. Jen was quick to my side with a comforting arm around my shoulders.

I felt someone kneel in front of me. "Don't worry. I'll talk to him. I've dealt with this before and can bring him around."

When I looked up, I felt tears rolling down my cheeks. The onslaught of tears blurred Kevin Bolden from my view, but I knew he was there. I recognized his calm and confident voice. Which was much stronger than my own when I choked out, "Thank you." I bent my head back down after I watched his blurred shape disappear out of the room.

20

Throughout the rest of the night, I debated going after Nathan myself. Well, let's correct that. It wasn't that much of a debate, and each time I tried, Jen or Marie either blocked me at the door, or distracted me in some way. Which wasn't really that hard in my current state. My mind was going in a hundred different directions all at once.

Speaking of my current state. There were two consensus in the house of where I was in that current state. Those that wanted to be sarcastic and take little shots at me, like Mike and Rob, who both agreed I was officially fat. Stan even got one in, and I had to remark that I didn't know shifters had a sense of humor. He promptly turned himself into a clown, and not a funny looking goofy clown. A horrifying fat clown with messed up teeth. He turned back when I told him I could freeze him like that. I wasn't sure if I could or not, but it was a nice threat, and he got the point.

Everyone else agreed I was between three and five months. It appeared I had progressed two months or more in just a few hours. There were no experts on this around. The only one that was familiar with the situation, albeit in reverse, was Theodora, and she hadn't been up to the house in more than a day. I had to assume she was out there with her beloved Marteggo.

I thought about sending one of the others for her, but I doubted she would actually return with them. I knew these thoughts Nathan was having weren't ones he came up with on his own. There was someone behind them, and his constant reference to the vampire pirate told me exactly who. That made me wonder. Did Theodora feel that way too? I wasn't sure. I remembered when we all sat outside at her place, while the elders discussed my problem. She said we are beautiful creatures that live a long life, and we should embrace all that life offered, or something to that effect. Could it be Theodora doesn't blend in as well as I assumed she did? Perhaps she lived more like a vampire than as a normal human. She had her own stock of blood, which I never asked how or from where.

I even visited my mother in the early morning hours, just to get her opinion. She guessed the same, but then asked me how many days it had been, stating the same the others said about how accelerated vampire pregnancies were. Of course, she couldn't tell me how sped up they were. How could she, or anyone, know that? It appeared I was the first, and I was getting really tired being the first or unique. I wanted to be like everyone else. My mother reminded me I was always different growing up and had that motherly smirk when she said it. I guess all parents see their children as different, or more special, than others. I just don't think she understands how bad it really was to be this different.

When the sun came up, I found myself on the porch, watching the edge of the woods for any sign of either Nathan or Kevin. There were vampires out there. Lots of them, and Marteggo was right there with them, watching the witches' camp again. It even appeared there were more vampires today than I had seen before, but that didn't matter. The two particular vampires I was interested in weren't among them. That didn't stop me from leaning against the banister for hours, looking until Lisa came out and asked if I was ready to go. At first, I didn't know what she was talking about, but then I remembered. Our next session with Mary Smith. If I could have skipped it, I would have. My mind was absolutely not into any training today, and especially not this. We almost made it off the porch before Amy caught us. I tried and tried to get her to stay behind, but even reminding her that yesterday was so boring that she fell asleep didn't deter her. She was insistent about coming and latched hold of my hand. In the end, I didn't mind. Feeling her there with me was the reminder I needed to take that walk and try to put everything else behind me. Jack made it rather clear last night he wouldn't be joining us. He seemed to lose interest after being told he didn't have the gift.

Mary was more welcoming today than I remembered her ever being in the past. She even greeted Amy with a hug when we arrived. She quickly ushered us back to the same room, repeating over and over, "we have a lot to do today." Now the biggest question was, could I focus on all we needed to today? Without being prompted, Lisa and I took our spots at two of the points on the pentagram. Mary didn't waste any time and produced the black candle. The smoke wrapped itself around the room in a single, continuous, string-like column.

"Today we are going to drift a couple of times. Each time will be further away from this place, pushing your limits with each trip. What I want you to develop is that feeling where you know where you are and how long you have been there. Then you can pick a place and time and drift to it, and you can find your way back. Now, close your eyes, and grab hold of the smoke. Do not let go of it for any reason."

I didn't know if it took me all that long or not before I felt it. I probably wouldn't know for sure until Mary told me. It was the same with how far I had drifted. I knew I wasn't within myself. I just didn't know really where I was. What was certain was the floating string of smoke was firmly in my grasp. I had even had it wrapped around my hand to make sure I didn't let go. Without Mary asking, I gave it a yank and returned to the room.

I opened my eyes, and I looked right at her. "So, how long, and how far?"

"You tell me."

I knew exactly what she was doing. She wouldn't tell us. She needed us to tell her. That was the whole point of this. I thought about it and realized I didn't have a damn clue. I looked over at Lisa, and she was still there with her eyes closed. Amy was looking through a book Mary Smith had obviously given her, but she wasn't asleep and didn't seem bored. That gave me something to work with. Not that it really helped me to narrow it down too precisely, and it wasn't exactly how Mary expected me to figure out how long I was gone. I knew we were within the range somewhere between an hour to minutes. So, I did all I could, and took a guess that lacked a lot of commitment behind it. "Twenty minutes."

She shook her head. "Try three hours, and you just barely made it out of the tent. Lisa, there has been out and back about nine times so far. You have this within you, but you need to do two things."

"All right. I can do that," I eagerly agreed, but maybe too soon. "What are they?"

"First, loosen up on the death grip you have on the smoke. Don't let go of it, but use it to move around. Pull yourself back and forth on it and treat every inch as a step. Judge your distance that way. Second, you need to focus more. Feel what is around you."

There was that word again. I hated that word. Each time someone said it, they were lecturing me about something I was doing wrong, and worse yet, they were right. I set myself to my task. Not really struggling to slip off. It seemed to happen pretty fast. Just as fast as last time, which I just heard took me hours. This time, I didn't wrap the smoke around my hand. Instead, I maintained a steady grip on it, and once I felt I had pulled free from myself, I reached up the smoke with my other hand, grabbed it, and pulled myself forward and released my other hand. It wasn't a big step, but it was still a step, and what a step.

I looked around through a translucent fog and realized the step I took was bigger than I thought. I was now looking down at the tent from fifty feet or more above it. Strangest yet, I could almost see through it. I could almost see through everything. Shadows and shapes hinted at what was inside each tent in the camp. I reached up the smoke again, and pulled myself up another length of my arm, and discovered I had a fear of heights. I was still above the tent, but now hundreds of feet above it. There was nothing below me except the little specks that were the tents, and the roofs of my farmhouse and barn. My feet kicked for the ground, but they just swung in the nothingness that was there. I had never been this high before, and I didn't really like it. I stayed there until I relaxed some. Once I had the nerve up, I wanted to explore further, but I didn't really want to go higher. I reached up and grabbed the smoke and pulled while hanging on with my other hand. I wanted to see if I could bend it, and wham, it bent at a spot just below my hand. I then messed with it some more. I could turn it in any direction I wanted. So, this is how I could move around.

Fascinating. I made a quick pull down it and I was now miles away, and a light bulb went off in my head.

Pride welled up inside of me, and I needed to tell someone. I gave the smoke a yank and zipped right back to my body. It happened too quickly for me to notice each of the previous times, but now that I was further away, I was aware of what happened, and I saw what was beneath me on my trek back. Below me, witches moved and ran through the camp. Strange, I didn't remember there being that many. I sank down into my body and emerged with my mouth opened to tell Mary Smith what I had experienced. The woman was nowhere to be found. I looked around and saw Lisa standing with Amy huddled behind her. Lisa had a defensive stance, and I heard explosions outside the tent.

"Thank god you're back!" screamed Lisa. "Get up! Get up!. The vampires are attacking us."

"What?" I screamed back. What she said didn't make any sense to me, but neither did the sounds of the war zone outside. I jumped up and ran out of the tent's opening. Several bodies laid on the ground just outside the tent. I had to assume they were witches. Screams and yells were all around, along with the sounds of explosions and impacts. I knew those were witches taking shots at the vampires. I didn't know why this was happening, but I didn't care.

Before I charged into the fray, I went back to Lisa and Amy in the back of Mary Smith's tent. Lisa started to ask, "What did you see– "

"You can't be here," I said, interrupting her question. Then spun up a portal and pushed her and Amy through before closing it. They were now back in the house.

I made my way back out of the tent and looked around. Another body now laid motionless on the ground with the others. He was a witch. There was no doubt of that. I loaded both hands with fireballs, blue ones, and went on the hunt. If I found a vampire attacking a witch, they were going to pay a price. Understanding why this happened would be a matter for another time.

It didn't take long to find the fighting. I recognized both the witch and the vampire, but didn't know their names. I didn't care, and I didn't wait. I hit the vampire right in the back, setting him ablaze. It didn't faze him. He turned his attention to me. With one hand, I grabbed him without touching him, and threw him out of the camp into the woods. The landing wouldn't kill him, but it might sting a bit. It at least removed them from the fight for the moment. I reached down and helped the witch up off the ground. She looked at me with frightened and frazzled green eyes. Why wouldn't she be? She had just been attacked by others that looked just like me.

"You're okay. I'm a witch–"

A strangely familiar slap in the center of my back interrupted my attempt to assure her she was not in any danger from me. It sent me flying forward, over the green-eyed witch I had just saved. My landing was not a graceful one. I just flopped on the ground, hard, but instead of popping up and returning the favor at whatever misguided witch attacked me thinking I was a vampire, my hands reached down for my stomach. It felt even bigger than before, but that wasn't why I reached for it. I was worried the landing hurt my child. That concern drove an uncharacteristic move on my part. I slowly sat up, with my hands in the air, turned around, and pleaded, "Stop. I'm not one of them. I'm a witch too, and I'm pregnant." I finished that plea before the shock of who I saw standing over me set in.

"Pregnant?" asked Miss Sarah Julia Roberts. "Now that's a gas. No matter."

I was about to knock her so hard it would send her back to the 90s where her dark stringy hair, leather boots, and mono-chromatic clothing she wore would fit in, but something pressed me back flat against the ground with my hands behind my head and held me there. No matter how much I strained, I couldn't move, roll, or twitch. Even odder, I couldn't witch. I tried. I tried everything from opening the ground below me to give me some room to opening the ground below her to scare her and make her release me, to floating away. Nothing happened. Then I realized she wasn't in control after all. A tall, sulking older man leaned over me from above.

"Don't bother fighting. You can't do anything now. Now come on."

My body floated up waist high on him and followed as he walked through the witch camp. Miss Sarah Julia Roberts followed.

"Let me guess, It's the Saxon boy's?"

I wasn't going to tell her, but I couldn't even if I tried. Whatever this was, kept me from talking and saved her from the barrage of insults I had lined up.

21

He paraded me around the camp slowly like some trophy kill strapped to his hood, except there was no hood. I just floated in the air immobilized. Out of the corner of my eye, I saw the bodies of witches everywhere. They were probably caught by surprise and didn't stand a chance against the vampires. With all that had happened over the last few days, they had probably dropped their guard. I know I had. I didn't see either camp being a threat to the other, but I was also not a good judge of that. Being both, I didn't have a clue why either was a threat to the other. It made no sense, but I remember Mr. Lockridge, the history teacher here in the New Orleans coven, once saying that wars never made sense. This one didn't, but it was clear who was winning. That was a lot clearer to me than the sides. At least two witches were helping the vampires, but why? This slow walk to wherever we were going, and the inability to move or talk, gave me a lot of time to think. Unfortunately, I found no answers. Just more witches that were injured or dead on the ground.

We finally stopped, and my captor tilted me up onto my knees, which bent all on their own. I thought this might have given me an opening, but there was nothing. No matter how hard I tried. Nothing moved. I tried a few spells and tricks, and nothing worked. Not even something as simple as setting a blade of grass on fire. There wasn't even a flicker or a spark.

My captor shook off his hood, revealing a pitted face and long dark beard. His dark eyes were hollow reflections of what I had to assume was a hollow soul. Physically, he was a mountain of a man, and cast a large shadow across me. He stood there, stoic, as if waiting for something. What? I didn't know. It was just him, me, and Miss Roberts. Or that was all I could see. If anyone was behind us, I couldn't see them. All I could see were those in front of me, and a shadow approaching. When I saw the source, I wasn't all that surprised. It was Marteggo. What I saw with Marteggo shattered me. Another witch, dressed like my captor, led a floating Marcus Meridian to my side, where they placed him on his knees just like I was.

"I believe this satisfies the agreement?" Marteggo asked.

Miss Roberts stepped forward. "It does. In return for these two enemies of the council, Jean St. Claire will never be set free. You have our word."

Marteggo grinned. "Good, but just remember what you see here today. If you fail to uphold your end of this agreement, it will be you next time."

"There is no need for that threat," barked my captor. He stepped in between Miss Roberts and Marteggo. I never thought I would see anyone larger that Marteggo, but I just did. He had several inches on him in both height and width. That didn't mean Marteggo backed down. He seemed to bow up and viewed the man as a challenge. It would be a one sided challenge from all appearances though. My captor didn't pay him any attention and turned to Marcus Meridian.

"I told you one day you would be a prize in my trophy case. I just didn't know I would add a second one." His blank eyes cut in my direction.

There was so much I wanted to do to him and Marteggo at the moment, but I couldn't. All I could do was think about all I wanted to do to them, but God help them when I finally get the chance.

"Wait!" cried a voice in the distance. "Marteggo, what the hell is going on?" I knew it was Nathan before he came around my side and reached down and tried to lift me up. No matter how much he strained, he couldn't budge me. I couldn't even move my lips to mouth any words to him. All I could do was move my eyes, which I darted in Marteggo's direction several times to tell him who was behind all this.

"Boy, leave my prisoners alone," barked my captor. He reached down and pushed Nathan aside, rather easily.

Nathan rolled on the ground and scampered to his feet. Then he got right in Marteggo's face. "Marteggo, tell him to let her go."

"I can't. We've made a deal that will keep Jean locked away forever," he said proudly.

"A deal?" Nathan asked, incensed. "Tell him to let Larissa go. Now!" Nathan shoved Marteggo with enough force to knock that smug look right off his face and send him stumbling back several steps. He recoiled right back at Nathan. Kevin Bolden forced himself between the two men and walked Nathan backwards.

"Nathan, don't take my company to mean your opinion matters," Marteggo sneered. He tossed his curly locks over his shoulders and away from his face. He composed himself, but was nowhere near the congenial person he always appeared to be. "I made a trade. Two fugitives for the council's help in keeping Jean locked away forever. It's for the good of everyone."

So that was it. That stupid decree Marcus had read to me a few days ago. That was why Miss Roberts and the other witches were here. He turned us in. That rat, that... he turned us in. No, that wasn't it. I corrected how I was thinking about the situation. The council knew exactly where we were and they could have come to get us at any time, but it wouldn't have been without a fight, and they knew that. Now the vampires, on the other hand... Yes, that was it. My mind put it all together. The vampires were the muscles. They gave the witches an opportunity to storm the camp and grab us. It was a battle of sheer numbers and force.

"Let her go!" Nathan screamed. Kevin fought like mad to hold Nathan back, but it didn't take long before Nathan got free and rushed at Marteggo again. There was no demand this time. Not that Marteggo was going to hear it. As soon as Nathan was within striking range, Marteggo planted his right fist into Nathan's head with a thud, sending Nathan to the ground.

I felt it. I felt every bit of that force against my own face, but there was nothing I could do. I couldn't even scream or beg Nathan to stop. He wouldn't have listened anyway. That punch didn't deter him, it only delayed him. He was up again, and this time delivered one of his own to Marteggo, and then to the two humongous men that had taken me and Marcus into custody. The strike sent both men to the ground, but not Marteggo. He stood there firm and didn't even flinch from the impact. Nathan punched him again, with all his might, and then I realized we were surrounded by the vampires as several rushed forward to grab and restrain Nathan, pinning him against the ground.

Inside, I screamed, "Get off of him! Let him go!" Nothing came out, adding to my panic as I watched this scene unfold. I screamed and struggled to get free. There was no way I was going to just sit here and watch them attack Nathan. The tears that rolled down my face told a different story. One where I didn't have a choice. Nothing worked. I couldn't even feel the vibrations of the world around me. I knew they had to be in chaos at the moment, but even then, I could have used them to do something. If only I could feel them.

Nathan struggled against the horde that seemed content with just restraining him.

"In time, you will understand," Marteggo said flatly.

Nathan spit at him in response, which prompted a chuckle from Marteggo.

"I believe our business is done here?" Miss Roberts asked.

"It is. Take them," replied Marteggo with a flip of the hand.

Two blurs knocked the group off of Nathan. He went after my captor first, but never reached him. There was a kind of barrier up. Not a rune for protection. Nathan would have felt that and kept going, no matter the pain. I could see that in his eyes. It was as if he hit a brick wall. Mike and Clay came out of nowhere and each made their own attempt to get to me, but they both hit the same wall. My captors didn't flinch on this side of the barrier as they watched the three make attempt after attempt.

"Go!" ordered Marteggo.

Neither of our captors appeared too motivated by that order. They lumbered back and gathered Marcus and me up off the ground. I was back to the floating slab of humanity with a full view of the war waging behind us. Kevin Bolden had entered it, and lightning bolts struck the ground, sending vampires scrambling. I couldn't see Lisa, but I knew she was out there. Marteggo stood there in the middle of

Armageddon, unfazed. Even the appearance of four large wolves snarling and stalking him did nothing for his demeanor. I recognized two of them, but then I remembered Marcus' guards. Their attack was short-lived. Marteggo stood proudly, almost laughing as they laid whimpering on the ground, as a large spinning portal opened up ahead of us.

I fought with everything I had to grab for the ground. To scream out to Nathan, or anyone. Nothing. I was just an observer of the most painful event I had ever seen. Everyone I cared for was fighting to save me, and losing.

Nathan walked through the wounded but once again stalking werewolves. "Boy, don't make me beat this stubbornness out of you. This is all for the greater good. Don't you see?" There was an edge to Marteggo's voice, a frustration. He rolled up the sleeves on both arms while the werewolves growled and nipped at him. A large fireball drove Marteggo to the ground, but not for long. He got up quickly, but it was just enough.

What I watched over the next few seconds sent shivers down my spine for several reasons. My head and body screamed, but I was the only one to hear it in my trapped state. Just before we entered the portal, I watched as Nathan leaped on the distracted Marteggo and relieved him of the burden he carried atop his shoulders, his head. Just like what happened to Mr. Norton. Marteggo's body slumped to the ground and turned to ash. Bits of it floated in the wind and the portal closed behind us.

22

We floated down a narrow rocky path carved into the side of a cavern that extended up as far as I could see. Marcus was behind me. One captor led us down the path. The other followed behind us. A fiery orange light from below cast ominous shadows on the craggy surface of the wall. We traveled down so far I eventually lost sight of the place we exited the portal at. I wasn't sure if we were at the bottom when we entered a dark cave that turned into a tunnel leading to another similar scene with a path that was nothing more than a wooden footbridge across what appeared to be a river of molten lava. Another cave or tunnel awaited us on the other side of the bridge. Beyond that tunnel was a cold, damp, and dark world. Hundreds of torches hung in the space overhead. They did little to chase away the shadows, creating points of light framed by larger spots of darkness.

We finally stopped at the end of a path that extended out into the middle of the dark cavern. Neither of the captors spoke. They stood together and motioned up in the air with their hands. Two of the torches above fell toward us. I watched as the flames atop them danced in the wind created by their movement. Two, huh? There were two of them. I made a wild leap that our two captors would use these torches to light the way for the rest of our journey to wherever. The closer the torches came, the larger they appeared, and more of our surroundings came into view. Large, winged creatures flew back and forth across the space. The flickering flames from the torches reflected against their slick and scaly skin.

I didn't have long to ponder what they were before the next amazing or terrifying sight came into view. It was the torches, which weren't torches at all. They were rooms or cages, with a blazing fire atop them. They both descended to the end of the path and their doors opened. Flames dripped down each side of the structure, disappearing into the darkness below. I floated into one of them, and Marcus into the other. Once inside the door, my body collapsed to the hard, cold floor. I could move again and I pushed up off the floor.

The captor that took me stepped forward and once again pulled the hood away from his face. "Welcome to Mordin. Save yourself the trouble. There is no escape, and there is no magic. Each cell cancels whatever spell you try. If you don't believe me, try it yourself. You will have plenty of time to experiment, as you will spend the rest of your life in this cell. Don't bother trying to scream. The cells are soundproof, not that anyone could hear you, anyway. The cell will take care of your basic needs.

Food three times a day, water, a bed for sleeping, a place to bathe, and clean clothes." With a flick of his wrist, the door on Marcus's cell closed and rose in the cavern toward its original spot. Our less than gracious host turned to and addressed me specifically. "Miss Dubois, we will monitor and provide assistance when it is time to give birth. We are not savages, but I am afraid your sentence also applies to your child, and they will serve that time with you in this cell for the entirety of its days."

"Wait! No!" I held both hands out to the man. "Don't do that. Let it live free."

He flicked his hand in my direction, and the cage door slammed shut, and up I went.

I collapsed to the floor of the cell and sobbed. Behind me, a simple bed with a single sheet appeared, but I settled for the floor. I needed something to pound against. Each smack of my fist against the floor produced no sound at all. The sounds of my own cries echoed back at me from the cage. I peered out, and the spot I had just left was no longer in view. There were hundreds of others of these cages dangling in the air. Some of their occupants were just going about their own business, sitting on the bed, or the floor, not reacting to anything. Others were watching me, the new arrival. I wiped the tears from my face and looked for Marcus. I couldn't see him in the sea of cages. He was out there somewhere.

One man with a mane of white hair on his head waved in my direction, and I returned a halfhearted wave. He picked up three pieces of bread and happily juggled them. I let my head collapse into my hands, and the tears rolled. This was it. This was where I was going to spend the rest of my life, except that was the problem. There was no end to my days. This was going to be forever.

23

 Forever was right. The only problem was days and nights were not two definitive times. There was no sunrise or sunset to separate each. There was just darkness surrounding the light illuminated by the flame atop our cages. Some slept while others were awake. Food seemed to arrive when you needed it, and not at set times. Mine hadn't arrived yet, and I was curious what would arrive when it did. Did this thing know I was a vampire? Would it? Could it? It already produced a bed for me, and I don't sleep. Maybe it was just so I could have a place to sit. Even more concerning, what would I do if it didn't know what I was? I couldn't exactly eat a ham sandwich if that was what arrived.

 A bathtub appeared later on the first day, and the water was lukewarm. For some reason I expected it to be just as cold as our surroundings. Not that the cage I was in was cold, or would get cold. I bathed while it was there and sat in the tub trying to let the warm water relax me, like it used to when I was a child. Come to think of it, I hadn't sat in a tub like this since when I was a child. The relaxation didn't come. My body didn't absorb the warmth of the water like I used to before. I didn't need it. Around me there were too many reminders for me to forget where I was, even for just the briefest of seconds, and I felt the tears flowing again, which made me mad.

 "Stop it, Larissa!" I yelled at myself. I wasn't the type to sit around and cry when something bad happened. Okay, I admit, calling this bad was a bit of an understatement, but still, that wasn't me. That wasn't me by a long shot. I was always the person who struck out. Either with words or actions. Why should now be any different?

 I looked at the walls of my cage. Small bars pressed closely together with just enough room to see through with little obstruction, but definitely not wide enough to slip through. If I were able to slide through, then what? I was hundreds, if not thousands, of feet in the air above that small path. They said magic wouldn't work here. Wait, no, that's not right. They said magic doesn't work in the cell. If I could get out, I could use it to float down? Something I imagine everyone in these cells had thought of, or tried at one time or the other. Why was I different? One fact pushed that self-doubt aside in my head. Because I am a vampire. If I fell, I wouldn't die. The others, if magic didn't work outside the cell either or was somehow limited, they would fall to a certain death. So, now how do I get out? I reached a hand out of the tub and grabbed on to a bar. I don't know what I was expecting, but I braced myself at first. There was nothing. It was nothing. Just a simple metal or iron bar.

"All right."

I got out of the tub, dried off, and put my clothes back on, which were remarkably clean again. I needed to test something. I walked right up to the wall of my cage and grabbed hold of two bars, one in each hand, and pulled hard. They didn't give. Not even a simple bow before snapping back into place. I tried again, and again. Then tried to push, hoping my augmented strength as a vampire would give me a slight advantage, or enough of one to spread them so I could slip through. There was nothing doing. These things were solid. So, I scratched that thought out of my head. What was next?

Ideas whirled around my head while I paced the floor. There weren't many, but there were some, and some was better than none. One particular idea kept being dismissed quickly over and over and yet kept coming back with the voice of my mother. "That's stupid," I mumbled to myself, and it was stupid, but that didn't make it a bad idea to try. There was no way to know for sure.

My mother once told me about why she exposed me to all worlds, both that of a witch and a human. In her explanation, she told me about a baby circus elephant that grew up with a single string holding its leg to a stake. As it grew up, the circus used the same small string and stake to hold it in place, even though the elephant was large enough to easily snap that string anytime it wanted to. They conditioned it with that restriction in place when it was young, and because of it, he would be forever limited by that string. She explained, only showing me one side of the world would restrict my view on the world and she didn't want that to be my string. Now that string had nothing to do with what I was thinking about, but the restriction did. What if they were bluffing about the cell canceling out magic? Like the string on the baby elephant. Establish a boundary we would never test. There was only one way to find out.

I stood in the center of the cage and tried to open a portal back to the farmhouse. I was glad no one I knew was around to see me achieve nothing but a sore shoulder, which even then I wasn't sure why it was sore. I shouldn't be feeling things like that. Perhaps this little bump I was carrying had something to do with that. Of course, using the word little wasn't that proper anymore. I was at least equivalent to someone that was six or seven months pregnant now. Its size grew exponentially every day.

Maybe something simpler, like setting the pillow I don't need on fire. That should be easy enough, or not. Nothing happened. Just like the first time I tried back at the coven, but unlike that time, nothing sparked out of my frustration either. At this point I would have accepted accidentally setting the entire bed on fire.

So, they weren't lying about that. There had to be something, some way. Something I wasn't thinking of. I went back to inspecting every inch of this cage for a weakness. Nothing was perfect. That was a statement I tried to believe while inside I begged for this to not be perfect. I climbed up on the bed to reach the top of the cage, hoping for a weakness up there, but another sensation sent me falling to the bed. There was a kick. A kick from inside. It was the weirdest sensation I had ever felt, and all I could do was sit there with my hands on my belly waiting for the next one, so I didn't miss it.

I didn't. I felt it do it again and again. It was such an amazing feeling. The feeling that there was life inside me. A life that I would do anything to protect. The bliss of the feeling gave way to a panic. I tried to fight back against it, but it finally won, sending me sprinting from the bed to the door, pulling as hard as I could. There was no way my child was going to spend their life in this cell. I couldn't doom them to that miserable existence. I had to get out. I had to. My hands banged and pulled on the bars, but they didn't budge. Even climbing up and putting my body weight into it didn't help. Maybe they needed something more forceful. I picked up the bed and tossed it at the closest wall. The bed disappeared before it hit the bars, and then reappeared right where it was normally placed. The cell was working against me. I threw both hands down to my side and screamed. All I needed was one more enemy.

Options were running short. I tried throwing the bathtub, and it returned to its normal place, full of warm water. Maybe something was perfect, and I just found it. Why couldn't my life be what was perfect? Or my relationship with Nathan? I collapsed on the bed, my once projectile, and tried to pull my knees up to my chest, but I couldn't. Something was in the way, so I just collapsed sideways and laid there, looking up at the top of my cage, watching the flames dance above it. I was sure somewhere in this place someone else was doing the same. With a turn of my head, I spied four others that were just lying in their cage doing the same thing, and those were just the ones I could see. There had to be others. There wasn't much else to do.

How much time had passed while I laid there, I wasn't sure. There were no clocks, and the passage of time never really registered with me. I couldn't tell you if I was sitting there for five minutes, ten minutes, or fifteen minutes. To me time was more of an anticipation. That excitement, or dread, I felt while I waited for an event to happen. Maybe it was meeting Nathan, or Mr. Norton coming home. Once the event happened, then it was about waiting for the next. It was the same way before I became a vampire. Looking forward to when my father came in from the field, for dinner, for the nightly family time. Now, there was nothing to feel anticipation for. There was no next event, just this.

I wondered if I could teach myself to sleep. That would be a great way to lose myself for some time. A break. Maybe I could dream. I had slept before, and had slept since, and yes, I was a human both times, but that didn't mean it wasn't possible. I just needed to let my consciousness relax, and possibly lose myself in one of my many daydreams. Make that my reality for a bit and allow myself to enter a trancelike state where I stayed for as long as I could. Just a few moments of joy out in the fields as a small child, or an evening with Nathan. Either could mean the world to me, to my sanity, which I had already wondered if I could keep it intact for the rest of eternity. I looked around and saw others sleeping and felt jealous. They made it look so easy.

To test it, I closed my eyes and took in the darkness. I laid there and tried to immerse myself into a daydream. Just a little fantasy, and while my mind entertained the idea and took in the other reality I had created, the actual reality was still there. I couldn't block it out. It was always there, and it was more than just a nagging. It was right upfront as a reminder that the other world, my created world, wasn't real. That didn't stop me from trying. I went back to my alternate reality for a while.

I repeated my experiment many times, and each time I ran into the same issue. The real world was still there, no matter how much I tried to leave it behind. That didn't mean I didn't receive some benefit from this, though. There was some relaxation that came from it, but that was short-lived. The minute I stopped, the reality of my situation collapsed down on me, along with the realization that none of that was real and that it would never be real again. I did a lot of crying after each time, but that didn't stop me from doing it again. I needed it, and when I considered an eternity like this, I could only hope to lose my sanity one day and remain in my fantasy world.

I thought I had done just that when I felt I was moving, but when I opened my eyes, I saw I was. My cage was descending, and those winged creatures I spied earlier were following it. Their yellow eyes stared through the bars at me. I stood up off the bed and moved to the door to see who was below waiting. There was a hooded figure standing there. Of course, there would be, and I doubt they were delivering good news. There was no pardon waiting for me. The only reason for the visit I could imagine was my child. A checkup of some type. Like my captor said, they weren't savages. My cage settled on the edge of the path, and the door opened under the watchful eye of the winged creatures. They hadn't come this close on my arrival and appeared to be watching me. Perhaps these were the prison guards. That thought made a little sense to me. They flew and roamed in the air just below where the cages floated. If anyone got out, they would have to fall through their airspace to escape. The only question left was, would we be a nice and tasty morsel for them, or would they put us back in our cage once they caught us?

I waited for instructions, but none were given. Instead, the figure, much shorter than my original captor, walked forward, and then grabbed me by the shoulder, and threw me out the door. I tumbled toward the ground, but never hit it. A portal opened up in front of me, and I fell into it head over heels until I landed on a wooden floor. A quick glance up, and I wasn't so sure I hadn't lost myself in one of my imaginary worlds.

24

"Mordin is no place for my grandchild to be born in," remarked Mrs. Saxon. She pulled the dark green hood off of her head, revealing her white hair and clear blue eyes. She leaned down to where I was on the floor, and placed a finger under my chin, and tilted my head up, and looked me over. "Are you all right?"

I nodded. That was all I could muster. My voice failed me. I felt like a little girl that was in so much trouble.

She tilted my head from side to side one more time, checking me over, and then gave me a yank forward. I collapsed into her and wept, and her arms wrapped around me.

"You're safe now."

"I'm so sorry," I blubbered.

"It's all okay." Her hand patted me on the shoulder, and then she pulled me in harder.

That was not the reaction I was expecting. I was practically responsible for the death of her son. Well, not his death, but he was now a vampire. I had destroyed so much of what she had worked for with the others. I had betrayed her and left the coven against her command, and my departure was rather forceful. Why this warm welcome? It didn't make any sense and made me feel uncomfortable. I pushed her back and looked into those bright blue eyes.

"No, it's not. I'm sorry about Nathan. I am so sorry about what happened." Tears continued to fall from my eyes. She didn't change. In fact, she had a little of a smile on her face. Now I was confused as hell. Which was how I felt the first time I came here.

Mrs. Saxon stood up and dropped her green robe to the floor, and offered me her hand. I took it and she promptly pulled me up to my feet and guided me over to my bed, where we both sat down. She, like so many times, crossed her hands on her lap, and sat up straight. I wished I could do the same, but the worry about when she was going to unload on me had me struggling to hold myself together.

"Larissa, it's all right. It's all okay." She stopped and then sat back even straighter than before. "Do you remember the first night we met?"

"Yes, the train." How could I forget what, at that point, was both the worst and strangest night of my life? There were other nights in contention for both titles now.

"Do you remember asking if your mother told me you were coming, and I told you I knew you were coming as soon as she put you on the train?"

I nodded weakly, clearly remembering that night and conversation, but my confusion was growing. Why was she bringing this up now? Why was she acting like this? She should be livid and trying to tear my head off. There was only one answer. I was right earlier. I had lost it, and I was stuck in my daydream, and that might not be all that bad.

"Larissa, I knew you were coming. I knew everything. I knew what you were. I knew what you were going to do. I knew you and Nathan were going to be together. I may not have known who you were," she tilted her head to the side. "I had to discover that along with you, and when I did, more of your future opened itself to me. I'm a witch, remember?"

"Divination," I whispered.

"Yes, so you have heard of it?"

I nodded again, realizing I must look like such a little girl only nodding in response to her questions. "Someone has been showing me."

"Wonderful," she clapped both hands together.

"Oh, I'm not very good at it," I blurted.

"Of course, you're not. It takes a lot of practice to master it, but you don't need to be great at it for the seven wonders. You just need to show you can do it."

"You know about that?" I asked, both surprised and worried. My special training with Master Thomas and Mr. Demius was supposed to be a secret. They both mentioned about keeping it from her, but now I wondered if she knew. Maybe she didn't. She never attempted to put a stop to it. Unless... I stopped my thought right there. It was as if a lightbulb went off over my head. A big ass lightbulb the size of the sun. If she knew. If she really knew everything, like she seemed to now, then she knew and let it happen. She may have even encouraged it, but kept it hidden from others to avoid anyone on the council knowing. What a sneaky little witch. I felt a little proud of myself for figuring that out. Now I hoped she was right.

"Yes, I do." She leaned forward. "And I can help you with that and the others. Which ones are you still struggling with?"

"Wait. Wait." I waved my hands and stood up. The realization I made pushed away some of the worry I had, and most of the confusion. Other confusion replaced it, but this was something that could be cleared up quickly. "Let me get something right. You have known all along that I was going to challenge Mrs. Wintercrest for supreme one day?"

Now it was her turn to nod, but instead of doing it slow and unsure, like I had been. She was confident and responding eagerly.

"Did you know about the training Master Thomas and Mr. Demius were doing?"

"It was my idea," she answered and sat back proudly. "We needed to know what you remembered, and what you needed to learn."

"But they said it needed to be a secret," I pointed out, hoping she would confirm what I believed. If she did, the cloud I felt in my head may finally evaporate.

"We couldn't let anyone find out. You never know who might tell the council. Which speaking of," she stood up from the bed and walked over to where I stood in the center of my room. She placed both hands on my shoulders. Any joy that was in her face before had left. This was the serious woman I had grown to know. "You need to stay in this room for a while. This isn't like before where I told you not to leave the coven. Many things have changed since you left. Mrs. Wintercrest is here, staying in a room down on the ground floor. Jean St. Claire is here, locked away in a room under her protection."

My body jerked toward the door. Mrs. Saxon's grip on my shoulders tightened, and I felt something else holding me in place. Something more magical.

"Larissa, there will be a time to deal with him in the future. That time is not now. There are bigger tasks at hand. Now, you can't even go up to the roof. You need to stay out of sight. We cannot have Mrs. Wintercrest finding out you are here." There was a knock on my door, and she let go of my shoulders and walked over and opened the door.

Mrs. Tenderschott rushed in and mugged me with a hug that pushed me back to the bed. "Larissa, I'm so glad you're home." She held on to me tightly and swayed back and forth. God how I missed this. Behind her walked in both Master Thomas and Mr. Demius.

"Marcus is settled in. He understands everything," Master Thomas reported to Mrs. Saxon.

"Good."

"You rescued Marcus Meridian?" I asked.

"Yes," Mrs. Saxon answered, looking back over her shoulder at me. "We rescued and retrieved everyone. Apryl, Mike, Clay, Brad, and Laura are back in their rooms. Amy is sharing a room with Cynthia for now."

"They seemed to have grown comfortable with each other," added Mrs. Tenderschott. I understood. I had seen the start of that myself.

"Steve and Stan are back, as are Rob and his brothers. Jack and Lisa are on the witches' floor, but isolated from the others for now. I am more concerned about one of the witches becoming suspicious or hearing something they shouldn't and then speaking to the council or Mrs. Wintercrest about it."

"Gwen," I muttered harshly.

"Yes, Gwen, or anyone else really, but yes, primarily Gwen." Mrs. Saxon pulled the chair out from the desk that I never used. She sat down and sighed. "Gwen is a good witch, and I don't doubt she would lay everything on the line for any of us.

Possibly even you, Larissa, but she also has ambitions for something greater, and that clouds what I can see of her future. Too many possibilities to play out. I honestly don't believe any of the others would, but I just don't know."

"They wouldn't," added Mrs. Tenderschott.

"I would hope that to be true," responded Mrs. Saxon. "Marcus is in a room that only I and Master Thomas have access to, and it will stay that way until all of this is settled, and he can be allowed out and possibly restored to his family's place on the council. Anyway, Marie Norton is just down the hall from you. Master Thomas, Mr. Demius, and I will continue your training."

"Stop," I demanded, rather loudly, startling everyone in the room. There was one name she hadn't mentioned. The only name I really wanted to hear right now. The only name that I thought would have mattered to her. "What about Nathan? Where is he?"

I watched as three witches immediately diverted their eyes from Mrs. Saxon and myself. This freaked me out. If there was good news, they wouldn't have reacted that way.

Mrs. Saxon sighed again and leaned back in the chair. Her shoulder slumped. "Larissa, you were in Mordin for seven days. During that time, I have tried everything I can to find Nathan. Kevin and Jennifer have too. We can't find him. After he killed Marteggo he disappeared with the other vampires."

"Tell her. She needs to know everything," insisted Master Thomas.

"Tell me what?" I asked, while I felt myself breaking inside. He was dead. I knew it. After he killed Marteggo, the others carried him off and killed him for killing their beloved leader. Oh God. My knees shook, and the room spun.

"We don't know anything for sure," she started, and I reached back for the post of my bed for support. "Jennifer and Kevin heard several rumors while they were searching."

"Oh, no," I cried.

"After he killed Marteggo, his followers began following Nathan. He seems to be the new leader down there, but those are just rumors. We don't know for sure, and we don't know where they went."

"We need to find him," I exclaimed. My hands instinctively went to my stomach, and all the eyes in the room followed. "We have to."

"I know Larissa. I want to find him too, and I will keep trying, but we also need to take care of you, and keep your training. Trust me. This all works out."

"How? How does this work out?" I asked. There were many answers to that question. It could be I give birth and raise the child myself as the new supreme. Nathan and I could end up together. Maybe we don't but he is part of our child's life. Those were only a few of the options. Hearing that it all works out, didn't tell me anything.

"Larissa, you know I can't tell you that. Just trust me."

Right then the baby kicked me from the inside, and I jumped, again startling the room. I moved my hand around to feel it do it again, and it did.

"You need to stay calm. The baby will feel the stress you feel."

I needed to calm down. No duh, really? Some things are easy to say than do, and that without a doubt was one of them. The weight of the world was on me, thanks to Mrs. Saxon and everyone else's master plan. Worry ate at me, and it wasn't taking little bites. This stuff was chomping away at me, and it continued to do so. I didn't even know I had anything left for it to chomp away on.

"Trust me." Mrs. Saxon leaned forward in the chair and reached over for me. Her hand landed on my leg. "This is all going to be okay. I can't tell you how. I can't tell you if everything is going to work out perfectly how you want it, or if there is even going to be a happy ending. What I can tell you is it all works out, and right now you need to focus on that baby."

"But I need Nathan," I whimpered.

"I know," she responded, and then her eyes left mine and arrived at my stomach. "I know you do. If I knew how to find him, I would bring him here to be here with you."

"I think I know," I said, and I did. If he was their new leader, there was a logical place to look first, and there were two people here that knew where that was, but I could only talk to one of them. "I need to talk to Marie."

25

Our welcome home party moved down the hall to Marie's room. If I was right, she was one of two people currently in the coven that might know where Nathan was. The other, I wasn't sure if I could be in the same room without trying to kill him, and there was the problem about getting past Mrs. Wintercrest to see him. Not to mention, I doubted Jean would willingly give up the information. Of course, there were a few potions that I knew of that would get him talking. I was sure Mrs. Tenderschott knew others, but she was more humane than I was and wouldn't opt for the ones that might torture him a little.

When we walked in, Marie jumped on me like so many have in the last few moments. It was a good thing I liked this sort of thing, or I might feel assaulted.

"We need your help," I said, and she stepped back away from me, but that didn't mean she released me. Her hands ran down my arms and gripped my hands. This was the Marie I have known for years. "Where did Jean keep you?"

She looked at me, confused every way the human face could. Tilting, skewed, and scrunched. "Why?" She looked around the room, searching the others for answers.

"We think Nathan got himself elected as the new leader of the New Orleans coven when he killed Marteggo. Where would they have taken him?"

"Kevin and Jennifer heard a rumor while searching for him," added Mrs. Saxon. "I think Larissa is right here."

I smiled proudly. "He must have had a house or mansion he stayed in. I saw the inside a few times when he projected into my head, but I never saw the outside, and I don't know where it was. If what they heard was true, they might have taken him there."

Marie looked back at me, not as sure about my idea as I was.

I shrugged. "It's all we have to work with." It was. I knew myself. I tried all the magic and spells I could find to locate Marie. The best I could do was find out if she was still with us or not. It wasn't until Jean slipped up and sent Clay after us that we had a window into his world, and I could see her. But even then, I didn't know how to find her. Well, there was another option, but that stack of books still sat in my room, and Mary Smith wasn't around to help me like she was before. I wasn't even sure if she survived the vampire's attack on the camp.

"He did. It's in the Fourteenth Ward, on Audubon. It's number 18 or 16. I can't remember. It has been so long since I actually looked at the number. I just knew where it was. You can't miss it. It's solid white, with large columns."

"Thank you." I spun around to Mrs. Saxon. "Just one trip. That's all I need."

Marie grabbed my shoulder and spun me back around. "You're not thinking of going there?"

I felt like a top spinning back and forth. "It's the only option."

"Larissa, you can't. You wouldn't make it ten feet in there without being killed."

Now it was my time to grab her shoulders. I looked right into her loving eyes and explained, "That was before. I have spent hours around all of them, and Jean isn't pulling their strings anymore. It's different."

That appeared to strike a chord with Marie, and many others in the room.

"He probably doesn't know I am free, or even alive," I said and turned to Mrs. Saxon. "Just seeing me will make him come back. I know it." I did. In my mind, the reunion had already occurred. He would run to me the moment he caught sight of me. Then he would take me in to his arms, and kiss me. Then all would be right with the world. Or at least that small part of it. At the moment, that was the only part I could fix. It was all that mattered.

"I don't know." Mrs. Saxon looked lost in thought. She was considering it, but something about the look on her face told me she wasn't a firm believer.

"I don't see any other way." Master Thomas both sounded and appeared indifferent about his vote, but I understood. I was believing with my heart this would work. He was thinking with his head. The only sure thing here was this was the only option we had.

"I agree," Mrs. Tenderschott stated. "I don't believe any other way. Plus, love can conquer all. No matter what has happened, once Nathan sees her, it will all change."

"Just one trip," I begged Mrs. Saxon. "I know the street. I can put myself right in front of the address and go right in. No one will see me until I am there." I looked right into those clear blue eyes, and added, "Please." Once this idea came to me, I didn't expect to have to plead so hard for her permission. This was her son we were talking about. I thought she would have jumped on any idea that could bring him home, no matter how big the risk or how miniscule the chance of success was. This plan had a high chance of working, at least in my opinion. I didn't see how it wouldn't. I saw how he reacted when he saw me being taken away.

"Okay," she agreed with her back still to us. "But you won't go alone. I want Jen to go with you, and," she stopped and thought, tapping her foot as she turned toward us. "I want another witch to go with you, too. Jack."

"Why not Lisa?" I asked. Not that I really objected to Jack. Any issues Jack and I used to have were short-lived, and we were rather friendly. He was one of a few that

I think really got me, but going in where we were going, if I needed another witch, I would prefer it to be someone who had dark magic on their side.

"I'll go," volunteered Master Thomas.

Okay, I'll accept that.

"I'm on the outs with the council anyway. If anyone sees me, there is no harm."

"All right. Master Thomas it is, but remember both of you, it is straight in, and back," warned Mrs. Saxon.

I answered, "Yes ma'am." I hoped Master Thomas didn't mind me answering for both of us. "I need to change first."

Mrs. Saxon agreed, and I headed to my room, which was just two doors down. I stopped and winced at my door. A sharp pain is such a unique sensation for someone who hadn't felt pain in decades. It almost sent me to the floor, but I recovered quickly and kept going. Another one hit me just before I reached my door.

Two doors back, I heard Mrs. Tenderschott volunteer, "I'll get Jen." The familiar sound of her steps started toward the door, and then emerged in the hallway. I grabbed hold of my door handle and forced myself to stand up straight. The pain hit again, but I shoved it back as deep as I could. It would have been easier if I could have skipped into my room before she passed by, but I was afraid to let go of the door handle.

Mrs. Tenderschott looked at me curiously as she hurried by. "I'll get Jennifer. It won't take me more than a minute."

"Okay," I forced.

When she finally made it out the door to find Jen, I collapsed to the floor, and reached up and pulled down on my door handle. It opened, and I slowly slithered into my room on my back. A flick of my wrist shut the door behind me. I tried to reach my bed, but I couldn't before another bolt of pain hit me. It took all I had to stifle a scream. Again, I reached for my bed and attempted to pull myself up by the spread. The pain was excruciating. Drops of moisture developed on my brow, and I felt both a great squeezing and pushing at the same time.

"Holy crap!"

I let go of the spread on my bed. There was no way I was going to pull myself up there physically.

With a palm placed flat on the floor beside me, I said, "levioso", and floated up, but another shot of pain hit, stronger this time, and I crashed down to the floor with a thud. I was afraid to move at that point. Every attempt I had made so far had resulted in pain. I move. I hurt. That was my theory. Why I was hurting was a mystery? Then my theory failed. I was sitting still and another shot of pain, more intense than the others, hit me, and a fist pounded the floor.

"Larissa, are you okay?" Mrs. Saxon asked through the door.

"I'm fine," I called back, half writhing, and realizing I wouldn't even believe myself. There was no surprise when the door burst open, and she rushed in.

"Marie! Mrs. Tenderschott!" she yelled back at the door. Marie showed up in an instant. Mrs. Tenderschott wouldn't hear her. She was probably midway down the stairs looking for Jen.

"Let's get her up." Marie bent down and cradled me in her arms. She didn't wait for Mrs. Saxon to help. She lifted me up on the bed.

"Is it too early?" Mrs. Saxon asked Marie.

Before I ever thought about what she was asking, I asked for her to clarify, "Too early for what?" I knew. I knew the moment I said it. I knew it the moment Marie placed her hands on my belly.

"No," answered Marie. She leaned down to listen and then sat up smiling. "Its heartbeat is strong; I feel and hear it. It's ready to come out and see the world." She turned to Mrs. Saxon and repeated something I had heard way too much recently. It still lacked the specifics I was looking for, and I knew Mrs. Saxon was too. "Pregnancies by a vampire are unpredictable. Sometimes it's weeks to months, but never the full nine months. Larissa is unique," Wait! Did I just see Mrs. Saxon smirk at that. I was about to call her out on that when another pain sent me bucking back against my mattress. Both women attempted to comfort me. It didn't work. "She is the only vampire I have ever known to become pregnant. We believe..."

"Magic," Mrs. Saxon replied. She looked down into my eyes. "Mr. Demius told me about the duck. Did that happen here? Is that what this child came from?" She asked caringly, but that didn't take any of the uneasiness out of my answer. She was the mother of the boy I slept with. She was assuming this was something I created out of my own desire. Now I needed to tell her what really happened. Another sharp pain shot to me, adding to the discomfort of the moment, and I groaned and screamed. That scream saved me from further unpleasantry.

"Mrs. Saxon, we believe magic only played a part of this. They conceived the child," Marie started, and then stumbled slightly as she approached the next part. She was doing a lot better at this than I would have. I would have choked on the first word. "Traditionally. Magic just added it. A loss of concentration, if you would."

The look between the two women when Mrs. Saxon finally realized what it meant was priceless, and I realized I had seen this scene in several movies and sitcoms. The mother of a girl, informing the mother of a boy, that her son knocked up her daughter. A classic on many levels. I just didn't enjoy being the main character when Mrs. Saxon looked down at me. I braced myself for some motherly comment, but there wasn't one. Her face lit up, and she bent down and kissed me on the forehead. "So, it's really his?" she asked in my ear.

"Yes. All his," I replied, and then I screamed again. That shot was the most severe yet.

"Well then, how do we do this? I wasn't awake when I gave birth to Nathan." She looked over at Marie, who just shook her head.

"I never had the chance."

"This would be a good time for some magic," I started and then finished with a scream.

"Is there a doctor you trust?" Marie asked.

Mrs. Saxon rolled her eyes. I knew what she was thinking. How exactly would you explain all this to the doctor? Hey Doc, we need your help to deliver this child. The mother is both a witch and a vampire, and she has only been pregnant about two weeks.

"Wait," she jumped off the bed. "There isn't a doctor, but we do have a nurse." She disappeared out the door, leaving me and Marie alone.

Marie pulled me up higher on the bed and let my head lay on the pillow. It was soft and really comfortable. I had never used it before, but I think I might find a way in the future. Then she yanked off my pant and covered me with a blanket.

"Let's do this." She bent my legs, putting my feet flat on the bed. It felt a little better. Not as much pressure. Maybe she knew a thing or two, but then I realized she was doing the same thing they do in movies, but she had missed two things they always ask for. She hadn't asked for boiling water and towels.

By the time Mrs. Saxon returned, Marie had me propped up and as prepped, as if either of us really knew what we were doing. The pain was coming strong and fast, and I had given up screaming with each impulse. Now it was just a continual groan. Seeing who walked in the door added to that groan.

"Larissa. Relax. Ms. Parrish was a registered nurse before she came to our world. She still tends to the scrapes and bumps of our students."

She didn't say a word or even cast me a look. She just took position at the end of the bed. I felt her cold hands and wondered if she would have warmed them up first if she had actually liked me. "Good, we can do this naturally," she said from behind the sheet Marie had placed up and over my knees. "How far along are you?"

Before we went through that explanation again, I answered, "About two weeks."

Ms. Parrish didn't miss a beat. She kept doing what she was, and replied with, "You're lucky. Shifters carry for three years before the baby is full term."

I let out a loud groan as another wave ran through me.

"Larissa, on the next one, I want you to push," she said.

In the background, a stampede came down the hall, and Mrs. Saxon flicked the door shut. "Classes are over," she said as Marie looked toward the door. "They won't be able to hear anything with the door shut."

"That's not what she is concerned about, Rebecca. There is going to be a lot of blood."

Mrs. Saxon snapped around. From where I was, I saw her hands move, and then watched both the door to the hallway, and the one to the closet staircase to the roof glow. She had sealed them with runes. There was no chance they were getting through that.

I craned my neck to the side so I could see around the sheet. "Mom," I caught myself, but didn't correct it. "Are you going to be okay?"

My question prompted a glance from Mrs. Saxon, and I felt Ms. Parrish stop doing whatever she was down there.

She gave a terse nod of her head in my direction and then glanced at the others. Tension filled the room, and I believed we were about a second from Mrs. Saxon zapping her to the other side of the door. Inside, I debated with myself whether to stop her. I wanted her there with me, but also knew the risk. Marie saved herself by remarking, "Who do you think taught Larissa her control?"

I heard two large exhales, right before my next wave of pain.

"Push now?" I asked.

"Yes, Larissa. Push hard," commanded Ms. Parrish. Her next order was for Mrs. Saxon. "Rebecca, I need towels and hot water. You think you can whip that up?" Before she even finished the request, both were there.

"Oh my," Marie said excitedly.

"What? What's wrong?" I cried.

"Nothing," said Ms. Parrish. "When I tell you, I want you to push again, and don't stop until I tell you. Got it?"

"What's wrong?" I asked. Something was wrong. I knew it. Why else would Marie have reacted that way? I craned my neck again. "What's wrong Marie?" She never looked at me. Oh God.

"Larissa," snapped Ms. Parrish. She looked up over the top of the sheet. A light sheen of red on her hand. I didn't even flinch at its sight. "Nothing is wrong, but there is going to be a problem if you don't do what I say. Now when I say, push, and don't stop until I tell you to stop. Got it?"

I nodded back, and she ducked back down behind the sheet. "Now push. Push. Push. Push."

I pushed with everything I had for as long as she said the word. The bedframe let out a loud crack under the force, and I felt it dip to the floor, but that didn't stop the order of "Push" and I didn't stop pushing, and then she stopped, and I heard the most magical sound in the entire world. A small little cry.

26

"Are you sure you're ready for this?" Jen asked as the three of us stood in front of the white columned entrance of 18 Audubon Place.

"Larissa, you just gave birth. Maybe take a day or two to recover," suggested Master Thomas.

"I have to do it. It's more important now than it ever was." There was so much more at stake. So much had changed in just the last few hours, and I saw the world through a different light. I needed Nathan. We both did, and every moment I delayed, robbed the three of us of those moments, those opportunities to be a family. "Not to mention. I'm fine. It's been what, two or three hours? That is weeks in my time. Remember, I just gave birth to a child that I took to full term in just two weeks."

I led them up the steps and to the door. Before we arrived, I had already debated whether or not to knock. I had decided not to, and twisted the handle, prepared to force the lock open, but I didn't need to. It was unlocked. The three of us walked into the large, spacious white entry. There was a staircase and hallway ahead of us, with hallways on either side. There were no heartbeats to follow, and no smell of fresh blood. Traces of old stale blood were everywhere, and smelled putrid to my senses. Jennifer noticed it too and walked around the room, checking.

I was about to just pick a hallway to follow when we saw movement in the one to our right. Two vampires that I vaguely remembered from the nights out in the trees came around the corner and slid to a stop when they saw me. They smelled or felt Master Thomas and wanted to make a quick meal out of the intruder. My presence changed the menu, and they ran back the way they came.

"This way."

Jen and I ran after them. Master Thomas followed the best he could. A few turns through the house, and the clean white look changed to something more old world. Dark woods and such. We passed a hall of French doors. The scene I saw through their glass insets caused me to do a double take. There was the ballroom from one of Jean's visits. We kept going until we reached what appeared to be a single hallway that all the others converged into.

We stopped there and waited for Master Thomas. I didn't want him to be alone for this part. Something about it felt ominous, almost like we were walking into the mouth of the beast. I couldn't say why. It was just a feeling with a few flashes of details. All I could see in them was a room at the end of this hallway, and a hideously large wooden throne. If only I had a few more sessions with James to fine tune this new skill.

We walked, keeping Master Thomas between Jen and me the whole way. The opening to that room was just ahead, and shadows flashed back and forth across the doorway. I was the first to step through the opening, with Master Thomas right behind me, and Jen behind him. This room felt heavy and matched every detail I had seen in the flashes except the wooden throne. I couldn't see it anywhere. We were not alone either. Most of the vampires I had seen out in the woods, following Marteggo around like a lovesick puppy, stood to our sides and before us.

"Where is Nathan? Where is Nathan Saxon?" I barked, hoping Nathan would hear his own name and come forward. Who came forward wasn't Nathan, and before this pale figure in a three-piece suit and top hat stepped clear of the crowd, he spoke to another, who took off running toward the back of the room. I tried to watch where he went, but lost him several times. I last lost him when he passed a staircase made of old rocks. The shape of magic changed at that opening. It was chaotic and dark. That was when I knew. That led to the mildew covered dungeon that Jean pulled me to in one of his visions, and where he kept Marie.

"You have a lot of nerve coming here after what your kind caused." The top hat gentleman looked right over me and at Master Thomas. "You should leave," he warned, and I felt Master Thomas take a step back. I reached back and grabbed him by the hand.

"Our kind," I said, emphasizing the first word for all to hear. "Shouldn't you be saying that to yourself? You attacked the witches' camp and killed how many of our brothers and sisters? I was there, remember?"

The man didn't even look at me. He stayed locked on to the only non-vampire in the room. I felt him attempt to back away again, and again I pulled him back in line. I wasn't trying to show solidarity with the only other witch in the room. This was for his safety. If we offered them any opening, he would be a goner before he had a chance. There were too many of them for one witch to fend off. Even too many for two vampires to fend off, but these had all seen what I did to Jean before Mrs. Wintercrest interfered. They knew not to push.

The man laughed, and those behind him joined it. Before, when I considered all the probable outcomes, having to fight our way out of this was not one of them, but that didn't mean I wouldn't. My legs hunched down a bit, and I let go of Master Thomas's hand to avoid hurting him. A red glow glared from my hands, and several of the vampires backed up. But not old Mr. Top Hat. He stood his ground right until another vampire pushed him aside and grabbed me, hugging me tightly. I even felt one of his hands let go long enough to give Master Thomas a pat on the shoulder.

"You're free. How did you get free?" Nathan asked.

"Long story," I said, and squeezed him tighter. Over his shoulder, I saw our welcoming party back up and disappear into the gathered crowd. "Your mother can explain. Let's go home," I said feeling a little weepy eyed.

"What? My mother? Home?" Nathan asked, confused, and let me go, backing up a few steps.

"Yep. Your mother rescued me and allowed everyone to return. Let's go home." I reached out for his hand, and he moved it away.

"Larissa. You should stay here with us. You and Mrs. Bolden. Master Thomas, you will have to leave." He backed away a few more steps.

"Don't be silly. Now come on." I reached for him again, and this time, not only did he pull back, but he also turned away.

"Nathan?" Jennifer stepped forward. I put my hand on her and held her back. This was my fight. She was only here for the muscle.

"Nathan, what's going on?" I walked forward to him and attempted to place my hand on his shoulder, but he shrugged it off as quickly as it landed.

"You already know. We have had this conversation before." He turned around. Any happiness he had about seeing me was gone. What was left was unrecognizable. "You are a vampire. Your place is with other vampires."

"Not this again," I huffed. Marteggo was gone. The source of all the crap that was filling Nathan's head had been cutoff. I had him pulled back. What happened?

"No, it's not this again." It was his turn to huff now. "It's not the same as before at all. It's all different. It's all different because of what your kind did." He first pointed at Master Thomas, and then at me. His other hand shot up over his head and snapped. "I admit, seeing the life in the coven, things look amazing, but there is a dark side to the world of witches that makes us look civilized. Master Thomas told you about the war with the rogues, and I saw it. That was the first in a long list of examples that show the true darkness in the world of witches. If it doesn't fit, they must rub it out. You saw how many rogues showed up on your doorstep the minute they felt there might be a power shift, but you didn't fit, and your own kind made a deal with us to have you and Marcus imprisoned."

"Nathan, that is not it. Mrs. Wintercrest sees me as a threat," I tried to explain, but he walked up to me and held a finger right up in my face. His gaze cut deep.

"A threat because you are different. Just like I am different. Just like we all... are... different."

"Nathan, you have it all wrong. It's not that. I am a challenge to her seat..." he cut me off again.

"It is that. You can't see it because all the whispers of saving the world Master Thomas and others feed you have blinded you from the truth."

"Nathan! You know that's not true. What I am doing is trying to fix all that. That is all Master Thomas and the others want too. And your mother is in on it." He turned his back to me, but I ran around him to look him right in the face. "You have to believe me. You know this is true." I pleaded, and placed both hands on his shoulders. Then I threw my arms around him, and waited for him to do the same, but I never felt them. I looked up, and he wasn't even looking at me, he was looking over me. "You have to believe me." I let go and stepped back so I could look up into his eyes. I needed to ignite that connection again.

"Tell me, did my mother know about this?" He reached behind him into the crowd and pulled back a fist full of gold chains. Blood charms of various shapes and sizes dangled at the end of the chains. "After we did the dirty work, and you were taken, the witches turned on us, killing thirty-seven of us. Why? Because we didn't fit in, even though we made an agreement with them. So, tell me, does my mother know about this? Let me guess, that bitch Mrs. Wintercrest is there in the coven with her."

I didn't answer. I didn't have to. My lack of a denial appeared to have told him all he needed to hear, and he exploded, thrusting the fist of chains toward me, stopping just inches from my face. "Take a good look! This is what the witches did to your brothers and sisters. They betrayed us. You have a choice to make. You can be with us, where you belong, or you need to go and never come back."

I had already made the choice, but felt too broken to make it known. There really wasn't a decision at all. There were larger things at stake, more lives, than just the two of us that needed to be considered, but that didn't make it any easier to say. The eyes of everyone in the room wore away at me, and the first tear fell, again. I had been crying a lot lately, for various reasons, but all of them paled in comparison to this. I had one more card to play. It had worked before, and I needed to play it again. I needed to get him away from here. Somewhere we could talk, and I could help him understand, away from all these influences that I knew were pulling his strings. They had to be.

"Nathan, come back with me? Come back and talk to your mother? See what she has to say and if you decided to come back..." I almost couldn't get this out, "I will send you back."

"Sure, you will," he marched away from me, and the crowd parted like the Red Sea. Back against the far wall, I finally saw it. The wooden throne, with lion's heads carved into each armrest. Nathan walked right up to it and sat with one leg slung over the armrest. The blood charms still dangled from his fist. "I go back, and you or her throw some runes up and I can never leave. I see how it all works. Sorry, we trusted you once, and this happened." He shook the charms. "Larissa, your place is here with me. We have a connection unlike anything, but I can't go back to that world, and you shouldn't either." He almost sounded tender and caring. Not the hostile person who had stormed around making claims for the last five minutes, but that was short-lived. "Now you have to decide. Stay here and live the life you are meant to have, or leave and be one of those backstabbing witches. What's it going to be?"

I threw my shoulders back and braced myself for what I was about to say. More for my benefit than for anyone else's. I didn't expect to be able to say it without breaking down in a heap on the floor, but it was the only choice.

"Well, what's your choice?" he leaned forward.

"I am both a witch and a vampire. I can't turn my back on either part of who I am," I said as calmly as I could. Inside, I was about dead.

"Then be gone," and with that, the crowd closed in around us. "Witches aren't to be trusted. You should know that better than anyone else. Remember how the council has treated you."

"I can say the same for vampires. Jean spent decades hunting me," I spat back, which was probably not the best of ideas in the mixed company.

"Go, you have made your choice."

My arm spun around weakly, and a portal opened to the coven. Master Thomas practically jumped through it. Jen went through but stood there on the other side, waiting for me. I stepped in with one foot, but stopped before I stepped in with the other. "Yes, I made my choice, but it is not because of you or them, Nathan. It's because of Samantha, our daughter, and she is a witch too."

I stepped through and closed the portal.

Up Next - Coven Cove Book 6 — Blood Wars

Pre-Order HERE!

Stay in Touch

Dear Reader,

Thank you for taking a chance on this book. I hope you enjoyed it. If you did, I'd be more than grateful if you could leave a review on Amazon (even if it is just a rating and a sentence or two). Every review makes a difference to an author and helps other readers discover the book.

To stay up to date on everything in the Coven Cove world, click here to join my mailing list and I will send you a **free bonus chapter** from "The Secret of the Blood Charm".

As always, thank you for reading,
David

A big thank you to my beta reading team. Without all your feedback, books like this one would not be possible. Thank you for all your hard work.

The House of the Rising Son © 2023 by David Clark. All Rights Reserved.
All rights reserved. No part of this book may be reproduced in any form or by any electronic or mechanical means including information storage and retrieval systems, without permission in writing from the author. The only exception is by a reviewer, who may quote short excerpts in a review.

This book is a work of fiction. Names, characters, places, and incidents either are products of the author's imagination or are used fictitiously. Any resemblance to actual persons, living or dead, events, or locales is entirely coincidental.

David Clark
Visit my website at www.authordavidclark.com

Printed in the United States of America

First Printing: February 2023
Frightening Future Publishing

Printed in Great Britain
by Amazon